THE
RELUCTANT
HERO

THE RELUCTANT HERO

•

Bernadette Pruitt

AVALON BOOKS
NEW YORK

PRINTED IN THE UNITED STATES OF AMERICA
ON ACID-FREE PAPER
BY HADDON CRAFTSMEN, BLOOMSBURG, PENNSYLVANIA

Chapter One

The house was the picture of perfect order. Freshly painted and newly fenced, it stood under a canopy of budding branches like a Victorian lady with her parasol poised over her shoulder.

But inside, the house was a wreck. And so was its new owner, Alison Perry.

"Mommy, somebody didn't put their things away," her four-year-old son, Alex, said. His voice echoed off the peeling walls.

Alison couldn't respond for sneezing. Dust was everywhere. What wasn't settled, danced in the afternoon sunlight streaming through the parlor windows. It covered the baby grand piano, a wooden ironing board, an old tricycle minus a pedal, a listing floor lamp, its shade yellowed and torn, a dress form, an army cot, an ancient electric fan with a missing blade, and something that looked like a prehistoric forerunner to the vacuum cleaner. It covered boxes of heaven-knows-what that came from heaven-knows-where. All Alison knew was that except for the piano and the furniture that had come with the house, none of this was supposed to be there.

She sneezed again, this time so hard that her head rattled. She grabbed the baby grand to steady herself, leaving a stark handprint in the dust. "We'll get it cleaned up," she said, pulling him close. "When I get finished with it, it will be nice and bright and sunshiny with lots of room to play in. It'll be home."

He looked at her with eyes that were round, blue, and filled with a child's apprehension of all things new and strange.

If there had been a mirror in the drab and fusty room, Alison imagined her own eyes would reflect the same expression. She'd come to build a new life for herself and her son as the owner of this soon-to-be bed-and-breakfast inn. But at the moment, it was an inn from which she wanted out.

She looked at the twisted mass of junk again and for a fleeting second, she thought she saw it teeter. Taking Alex's hand, she stepped back, sneezing once more.

The house was in historic Cimarron, Oklahoma, a town she'd fallen in love with as a child during a family vacation. Her father had been transferred frequently, leaving her feeling rootless and without a sense of place. There was something about Cimarron, with its almost Disney-esque Victorian architecture, brick streets, cupolas, and turrets that answered a need within her. Widowed and in need of a way to earn money without sacrificing too much time with her son, she began searching for the right house in the right place. She found the house in Cimarron.

Inside, it hadn't looked so bleak when she'd signed the papers to buy it. It had been filled with furniture and knickknacks then, things belonging to Lura Bea Yale, a ninety-year-old eccentric who had taken up a new residence—in the town cemetery.

When she first saw the house, it had an air of shabby elegance to it. The drapes were old and heavy, but well made. The Oriental carpet was faded to a muted patina. The Chippendale sofa was threadbare but had a good foundation. The furniture came with the house. In addition, the old Victorian, which had three stories if you counted the attic, had what her German grandmother called *Gemutlichkeit*—a certain coziness, a sense of well-being. It was the perfect candidate for a bed and breakfast inn.

Now, most of the furniture had been pushed aside and the Oriental rug rolled up. Where the rug had been was a dark, plate-sized stain on the oak floor. The woodwork was in clearer view, its gouges and scars exposed, and Alison noticed that one of the windows was cracked. When she pulled back one of the drapes to inspect it more closely, the fabric, sun-damaged and rotten, fell apart in her hand.

She looked up and then noticed the water stain on the ceiling. She backed off warily to study it. The wavy brown edges were somewhat faded, meaning— she hoped—that the leak had been fixed long ago.

She turned back to face the pyramid of junk on the parlor floor. She'd take each problem one at a time.

Alison wasn't a gambler, but her circumstances called for something drastic. She had been left with a child who needed her more than ever, who was beginning to strongly feel the absence of a father. So she'd invested a good part of the proceeds of Kevin's life insurance policy in the quaint blue-gray house with red-and-white accents, turret, and a graceful wraparound porch.

It had character and charm and another plus: It was a good distance from the Texas air base where Kevin had died, making it easier to forget the past. And it was in a town where tourists came to see more than two hundred buildings on the National Register of Historic Places.

She strolled through the rest of the house. The dining room was bathed in a soft light from windows on two sides. In it was a long oak table, ten matching chairs, a buffet and a hutch. Over the table hung a chandelier, its crystals dulled from dust and time.

But the kitchen, with its vintage refrigerator and tiny apartment-sized stove, was a sad sight. Ancient asphalt tiles, which had been concealed by an assortment of rag rugs, buckled in front of the sink. And there was the unmistakable "plink" of a dripping faucet. She tightened the handles with a vengeance, but as soon as she turned to leave the room, the faucet mocked her with one more impudent drip.

The bedrooms were in better shape, although not by much. There were five of them upstairs, divided by a long hallway. Most contained dark and heavy furniture—not the kind she liked, but it would have to do for now. The small bedroom across from hers would be Alex's. The others would be for guests.

She climbed the stairs to yet another floor where there was a finished attic with small windows and a large closet. She'd promised Alex, who had been fascinated by the third-story view of the street below, that it could be his playroom.

She made her way quickly down the stairs, pausing at one of the house's most appealing features—an oval window, a Victorian oculus, on the stairway landing. Looking through its leaded glass renewed her hope and energy.

When she returned to the parlor, she found Alex asleep on the old sofa, his lips parted slightly and an arm dangling off on one side. Her heart gave a little twinge as she gently lifted his arm and placed it beside him.

After the long drive from Texas, she was tired too, but a nap was a luxury she couldn't afford. Her plan was to open the inn by May 15th—eight weeks away. Her first task lay in front of her—clearing the mysterious assortment of junk from the parlor.

It appeared that Lura Bea Yale hardly ever threw anything out. In the clutter were magazines dating back to 1947, bits of twine, a chain of paper clips, dried corsages, and candy boxes. Alison opened a heart-shaped box with a mangled bow and found a collection of cards and letters inside, some with postmarks dating back thirty years. But in the mix was a crisp, white envelope that had been mailed only two years ago from nearby Oklahoma City. It was addressed to Lura Bea and bore the auspicious return address of the Federal Bureau of Investigation.

Too curious to resist, Alison slipped the letter out of the unsealed envelope.

Dear Aunt Lura Bea,

Thank you for the tea and cookies. It's always a pleasure to visit you and I regret that because of my work, I can't do it more often.

Concerning your conviction that your house is haunted: I wish I could help put your fears aside, but I can't find any evidence of a ghost. It's simply out of my realm. Ghosts don't leave fingerprints or DNA and nobody has ever caught one, not even the FBI.

I know I'm disappointing you, but I'm sure there's a logical explanation for the things happening at your house. In time, I'm sure that the answers will present themselves. In the meantime, don't be frightened. I'm as close as the telephone."
Your nephew, Agent Stefan W. Yale.

Alison slumped to the floor, stone still. The room was so quiet that she could hear Alex's soft breathing. Nobody had said anything about a ghost, especially not Mr. Coury, the real-estate agent, who had been in such a hurry to get her to sign the papers. As for Lura Bea's heirs, she hadn't met a single one. The real-estate transaction had been done through overnight mail service.

She looked at the envelope again. At least this Mr. Yale had put his own stamp on it and hadn't used the FBI postage meter for his private mail.

Of course, she didn't believe in ghosts either. But just what were those things "happening" in the house? She took an uneasy breath. The stains, the leaks, and the buckled tiles had been surprises enough.

The next morning, as soon as the serviceman installed their new telephone, Alison called Stefan Yale. A harried-sounding secretary said he was "unavailable at the moment" but that she was welcome to leave a message. Since he'd had so many calls that morning, she wasn't sure when or if he'd be able to respond.

Undeterred, she left a message anyway: "Please call Alison Perry, the new owner of your Aunt Lura Bea's house."

He didn't call back. Alison went to town to rent a wallpaper steamer and to buy painting supplies, but there were no messages on the answering machine. Outfitted in overalls, a faded red sweatshirt and old sneakers, she spent the day attacking the parlor with the steamer and scraping her way through three layers of wallpaper. While she worked, Alex amused himself with the broken tricycle and an old Halloween costume found in one of the boxes in the parlor. It was composed of a black hat with a skull and crossbones on the brim, an eye patch, a peg leg and a plastic sword.

Just after five o'clock Alison, exhausted and covered with sheds of sticky wallpaper, collapsed on the piano bench to study the wall she'd just finished. An alarming crack in the plaster had been covered over by the latest layer of wallcovering—a flocked fleur-de-lis design faded to the palest green. Her gaze followed the crack along its menacing diagonal path from the ceiling to the floor. What if the house was structurally unsound, on the brink of snapping right in two? She was contemplating that grim possibility, her heart in her throat, when the doorbell rang. As she jumped up to answer it, the ring ended with a peculiar sizzle.

The hinges groaned as she opened the door. Standing on the porch was a neatly suited man, tall, dark haired and solidly built. His gaze, which shifted to her right cheek, contained a flicker of amusement. His initially stern expression softened into a barely suppressed smile.

Alison self-consciously felt along her face and picked off a stray bit of wallpaper. "Enjoying the view?" she asked with a prickle of annoyance.

His mouth tightened into a straight line. "I'm Stefan Yale," he said, ignoring the question. "The secretary gave me your message. I live nearby. I thought I'd stop by on my way home from work."

"Oh, yes," she said awkwardly, "please come in but watch where you step. You could end up papering the soles of your shoes." She briefly introduced Alex, who peered up at him from his one exposed eye. His other was covered with the black eye patch that went with the Halloween costume.

Stefan bent down and shook the boy's hand, then took hers. His grasp was strong, yet gentle, sending an unwanted tingle up her arm. He released her hand, then flexed his fingers. "Something's sticky."

"Oops, sorry," she said, jerking a paper towel off a roll sitting on the piano. "It's the old wallpaper paste. The steamer turned it back to goo."

"I'm sorry about your doorbell," he said, slowly wiping his fingers. "I think it fritzed out when I rang it."

Alison winced. "That too?"

A puzzled look crossed his face. "What do you mean?"

"Never mind," she said, not wanting to recite her troubles in front of Alex. "What I called you about . . ." She stopped in mid-sentence, then sent Alex out to try the porch swing in the springlike weather. She hoped there wasn't something wrong with it too.

When she stepped back inside, Stefan was leaning against the piano with his hands in his pockets and one ankle crossed casually over the other. One corner of his mouth was hitched in a slanted smile.

She parked her sticky hands on her hips. "What's so funny?"

For a moment, he said nothing. He simply studied her and she took the opportunity to inspect him back.

He was tall, all right, an inch or so over six feet, with a lean build that was solid, muscular, and toned to perfection. He was suited in dark gray, with a crisp, white shirt and a conservative dark green tie with a print. He wore his clothing with ease, not like a man who put on a suit only for special occasions. She guessed his age to be in his mid-thirties.

His hair was thick, straight and black, his eyes more gray than blue, eyes that seemed to be able to see right through her, leaving her feeling ruffled and exposed. His jaw was handsomely angular and his bottom lip had a stubborn but sensuous curve to it. He had a strong chin with an oddly charming horizontal crease. He was quite handsome, despite a nose that seemed to be a half-size too large for his face. It had been a long time since a man had been able to distract her in such a way.

"Tell me what's so amusing," she demanded again.

"When a woman offers a man a marriage proposal, you would think that she'd at least comb the pieces of wallpaper out of her hair and wipe that streak of dirt off her face."

Her heart bounced against her ribs. "What are you talking about?" Her voice was reduced to little more than a squeak.

He smoothly took a square of pink paper from his inside breast pocket and held it out. She snatched it out of his hand.

"And it looks like there's an added dividend, he said, turning and looking through the window at the boy in the porch swing—the little pirate."

Her mind reeling, Alison turned away in an effort to concentrate. The message read *Time: 9* A.M. *Caller: Alison Perry (new owner of aunt's house) Message: She wants to marry you.*

She spun back around to face him, her mouth wide, her tongue frozen.

"I'll understand if you've changed your mind. I'm a big boy. I can take it. The truth is that I'm very happy single and I intend to stay that way."

She shook the piece of paper at him. "This is a mistake. This isn't the message I left. Why would a woman want to call up a complete stranger and ask him to marry her?"

He shrugged. "I'm not sure, but it has happened to me several times in the last day or two."

Alison stared at him uncomprehendingly. "Why would anybody want to marry you?"

His jaw hardened into a slightly affronted look.

She touched her fingers to her lips. "Sorry, I didn't mean it the way it sounded."

His expression softened. "Sounds like I owe you the apology. Let me explain. I was involved in solving in a kidnapping case two days ago. The media made it sound like more than it really was. Women started calling and asking if I was married. Obviously, the secretary got some messages mixed up."

"You're right about that. I don't go around asking men to marry me."

"I'm truly sorry about the misunderstanding." His tone rang with sincerity.

She gave herself a moment to cool off. "Apology accepted."

Then the broader meaning of what he'd said punched a rivet of alarm through her.

"What were you saying about a kidnapping?" She

dashed to the window, where she could see Alex thumping around the porch with the peg leg that he'd managed to strap on.

"Don't worry," Stefan admonished. "The kidnapper has been caught. You haven't heard?"

"I just got here yesterday."

"That explains it then."

"What happened?" she asked.

"We caught a kidnapper," he said.

Alison sighed in frustration. "You could fill in a few of the details, you know."

He straightened to his full height and stepped away from the piano. "It's over. There's nothing to say. The bad guys are in jail. The child is safely at home with his parents."

"Child?" Her voice was filled with dismay.

Ignoring her, he pulled a handkerchief from his pocket, dipped it slightly into a pail of water that she'd been using to wipe down the walls, and took a long stride toward her.

"Be still," he said, taking her chin between his fingers. He angled her cheek toward him and gave it a thorough but gentle scrubbing. He was so close that she picked up his clean, male scent, one that made her think of freshly cut wood. He was so close that it made her heart gallop. "There," he said, suddenly releasing her.

Her face tingled. It might have been casual and meaningless, but it was a man's touch, something she'd grown unaccustomed to. "You didn't answer my question," she said, slowly returning to her senses.

A stubborn crinkle appeared in his chin. "I don't intend to. I don't talk about my cases. Besides, you'd just worry, and there's nothing to worry about. Tell me why you called."

She glanced through the window again at Alex. This time he was sitting on the swing, sawing on the arm of it with his toy cutlass.

"I called because I wanted to talk to you about your Aunt Lura Bea's house."

"It's all yours now," he said smoothly.

She tensed. "I'm afraid to ask what you mean by that."

"I was just stating a fact."

She looked at him warily. "I found a letter you'd written to your aunt a couple of years ago. She seemed to be convinced that this house is haunted."

There was a beat of silence. "She was at that," he admitted finally. "But you have to put it into context and consider the source. Aunt Lura Bea—she was my great-aunt, actually—was an institution here. With her white gloves and big hats, she was the last living embodiment of Cimarron's Victorian past. But at the same time, many people thought that she'd gone around the bend.

"For instance, she'd outlived all her old friends, but she continued to send them written invitations to her tea parties as if they were still living. That they didn't show up didn't faze her. The party would go on just the same. She would talk to them as if they were there." His resonant baritone filled the empty room, its tone somber.

"I'm sorry," she said. "If I'd known, I wouldn't have bothered you."

"You don't believe in haunted houses and such things, do you?" he asked. One sleek, black eyebrow lifted teasingly.

Alison felt her cheeks color slightly. "No, of course not. But the letter did mention something about things occurring in the house and, well, I'd like to know what they were."

Stefan stroked his chin. "Well, let's see," he said, pacing back and forth across the floor. One of the oak planks groaned. "Aunt Lura Bea said she heard noises in the night and that she felt odd drafts. I reminded her that there could be any number of logical explanations, one being that the house is over one-hundred-years old. Wood expands and contracts. Walnuts fall on the roof from the tree in the backyard. Stairways create drafts."

Alison began to breathe easier. "What did she say?"

He touched a hand to the back of his neck. "That satisfied her for a little while but then she started to complain that sometimes things 'moved,' that they weren't where she left them. Her stamp-collection books would be taken from the shelf and somehow left open on a table. There would be sheet music on the piano that she didn't remember putting there. There were logical explanations for those things, the main one being that poor Aunt Lura Bea was ninety years old. But that was one explanation that she was not willing to accept.

"I had one of the local cops make a sweep of the

rooms every night before she went to bed and that helped put her at ease, but she never gave up on the idea that there was a ghost in the house."

Alison frowned.

"You're not hearing things that go bump in the night, are you?"

"Things that go drip in the day. The faucets leak."

"I imagine they would." With his hands in his pockets, he paced around the room, surveying it from top to bottom. "In her later years, Aunt Lura Bea was one for letting things go. I hope you've got plenty of money to pour into this place."

Her stomach jerked. "What do you mean?"

"It's old. Everything about it is old and probably on the brink of failure—the wiring, the plumbing, everything. Now, even the doorbell is gone."

"Thanks to you," she said. "But it can be fixed and so can everything else."

"I don't doubt that. When are the crews coming in?"

"The who?"

"You know. The work crews—the plumbers, the carpenters, the electricians, etc."

"There are no crews, there's just me."

His eyes widened. "You're going to tackle this all by yourself?"

She picked up a wallpaper scraper and took on a menacing pose. "Of course. Anything wrong with that?"

His gaze swept over the room again. "When do you plan to finish, in a light-year or two?"

She cast him a curdling look. "May first, to be exact."

He regarded her skeptically.

"Look, I know I can't do every room by then, but I can do the ones the guest will use. It's going to be a bed-and-breakfast."

"Yes, I heard. I wish you well."

"Thank you," she said curtly. "It's time you said something encouraging."

A mirthful flicker appeared in his eyes. "All good things come to those who wait," he said, turning toward the door.

"Before you go," she said, "let me repeat once more. I did not—propose to you."

He stepped out onto the porch, then turned back to face her. "Good, because if you had, I would have had to disappoint you."

With a indignant tilt of her chin, she stepped past him, pulled Alex inside the house, and closed the door with a dismissive snap. She fastened the latch, threw the dead bolt and hooked the security chain.

That would teach him to come around again.

Just after midnight, Alison fell exhausted into bed. Despite the fresh sheets and the breeze coming through the open window, an oppressive fustiness hung in the air. She was almost too tired to care except that she couldn't sleep. Still in a fit of pique, she couldn't stop thinking about Stefan Yale's visit. She had a feeling that he would have behaved better if Aunt Lura Bea had been around.

Maybe he didn't have much faith in her plan, but she did, and that's what counted. In two months, she'd have him over for tea just to make her point. Then, suitably given his comeuppance, he'd be taken permanently off her guest list.

She wanted to raise Alex in a small and charming town and Cimarron had that Huckleberry Finn quality to it—a sense of permanence that would do a small boy good. For Alex, she'd do anything, even if it meant working eighteen hours a day, just as long as they could spend their days together. She would make something out of this place.

But while she lay in bed wanting to strangle her all too self-assured visitor with his own tie, she couldn't ignore the strong, masculine presence he'd radiated, one that apparently had drawn some women, however foolheartily, to approach him—figuratively at least—on bended knee.

And there was something else about him that stirred her. Maybe it was the way the playful sparkle in his eyes betrayed the stern set of his jaw, or the way his eyes seemed to peer right into her soul. It was a feeling that she hadn't had since Kevin died and it scared her.

She hadn't realized that she'd at last drifted off to sleep until she felt something on her shoulder. She sat up with a start, her eyes fluttering open in the darkness. Beside her was Alex's small form.

"Wake up, Mommy," he said, his tone anxious and pleading. "I heard noises."

Chapter Two

She scrambled into a sitting position. In the moonlight streaming softly through the open window, she could make out the shadowy features of her child's face. His eyes glistened with fear.

"What did you hear, sweetheart?" she asked, touching his shoulder. She could feel the stiffness in his small body. The cavorting cartoon characters on his pajamas contrasted oddly with the tension in the room.

"It sounded like somebody walking around my bed."

Alison felt a tightening in her chest. "It was probably just a dream." She tried to sound as calm as possible.

He shook his head adamantly. "No, Mommy. I heard something."

She switched on the lamp next to her bed and threw back the quilt. "Come on. Let's go look."

She took his hand and led him into the small bedroom just across the hall from hers. His favorite blanket, a worn blue fleece with a satin binding, lay rumpled on his bed, but everything else was in perfect order. There were no open books with pages that a draft could have stirred. There were no objects on the floor that could have fallen and made a noise. Alex had always been an extraordinarily neat child who kept his books and toys exactly in their places.

She examined the window shades, which were yellowed and brittle with age, and the windows to check for drafts that could have caused the shades to rattle. One window was open just a crack at the top, frozen into position from layers of old paint. She could feel a slight stirring of cool air.

Just to satisfy a small boy's imagination, she looked under the bed, finding nothing but a thick layer of dust, and opened the closet. It was empty except for a few cardboard boxes in which some of Alex's things had been packed.

"See, there's no one here," she said. "Do you know what I think? I think a draft caused the window shade to move. There's nothing to be afraid of."

"But I heard steps," he insisted.

"You *thought* you heard steps," Alison said in her best brave, invincible-adult tone. "When we're sleeping, things aren't what they seem to be when we're awake. Now, go back to sleep. Everything is all right."

She picked him up, tucked him and his teddy bear back into bed, and kissed him on the forehead. Although she'd pinpointed a plausible reason for the noises, she remained secretly unsettled.

"Alex," she said, looking into his clear blue eyes, "when you were playing in the porch swing today, could you hear Mr. Yale and me talking?"

His eyes narrowed. "Nope."

She was unsure whether or not to be relieved that he hadn't overheard them discussing Lura Bea's ghost.

"What were you talking about?"

"Well, we talked about the house. It belonged to his aunt."

Seemingly unimpressed, Alex yawned widely.

Alison gave him a quick kiss. "Good night, Tiger. "Sweet dreams."

But her own dreams were not so sweet. It was unlike Alex to wake up frightened, even in strange places. Even after the death of his father, he wasn't prone to nightmares and sleepwalking like some children.

Alison lay quietly, listening carefully for the slightest squeak or bump, but all she heard was the ticking of her alarm clock, a rhythmical, hypnotizing beat that seemed to mimic her own pulse. She refused to allow herself to believe that Lura Bea's claims had any validity, that there was anything at all to fear. But that night, she dreamed that she was trying to kick her way out of a soggy tangle of wallpaper that had come to life and twirled itself around her.

The morning sunshine was a perfect antidote to the dark rumblings within her. It had the soft, golden glow of spring, although spring was officially three weeks away. It lit up the windows and danced along the floor.

It reminded her that even the depressing old kitchen, with its maroon-and-tan tiled floor and chipped tan cabinets, was full of sunny possibilities. In time, she hoped to be able to afford bright, new black-and-white tiles, new white cabinets with glass fronts, and a sleek chef-style range.

Alex, who was finishing up a bowl of oatmeal, scarcely mentioned having awakened during the night. Instead, he talked of getting his own swing in the backyard, a tire that hung from a tree.

After breakfast Alison set Alex up at the dining room table with a new coloring book and crayons. She'd just filled up the wallpaper steamer again, and her muscles were sore from the day before. There was a knock on the front door, and she opened it to find a chubby middle-aged woman with a dark-haired boy of about five. The woman, outfitted in a sweatsuit and running shoes obviously worn more for comfort than for athletic pursuits, carried a covered casserole. The child held a small plastic dinosaur.

"Hi, I'm Rosalie Hightower from the gray house next door and this is my grandson, Mikey. We've come to welcome you to the neighborhood."

Alison opened the door wider and introduced herself. "This is so nice of you. Please come in."

"I rang the doorbell, but nothing happened," Mikey said.

As she told the brief tale of the bell's demise, Alex appeared, giving Mikey a once-over. Then he smiled shyly.

The grandmother, her short salt-and-pepper hair arranged in a cap of tight curls, whispered something in Mikey's ear.

"Broughtcha something," Mikey said, holding out the tiny race cars.

Alex's face brightened as he examined them. "Wow, thanks."

Rosalie held out the casserole. "It's tuna noodle. It's nothing fancy, but it sure tastes good when it's there fixed and waiting for you after a hard day."

Alison accepted it with gratitude. "Please stay for some coffee. I've got chocolate milk for the boys."

They sat in the dining room, leaving the children in the kitchen to spread their cars out on the old pine table.

"You're the first neighbor I've met," Alison said, setting a tray of coffee, cream, and sugar on the table. Alison had been amazed to find that the china, painted with periwinkles, had also been left with the house, although some of the pieces were cracked or missing.

"I couldn't help but notice, but it looks like you and Stefan Yale have met."

"Collided might be a better word for it," Alison said.

Rosalie looked at her quizzically.

"It was a collision of personalities."

The older woman set down her cup. "This is a first. Stefan tends to have the opposite effect on women."

"He told me that in so many words," Alison said dryly.

Rosalie's eyebrow lifted slightly. "You're probably the only woman in Oklahoma who doesn't think Stefan Yale belongs on a pedestal, except for the man himself." She twisted her mouth as if in thought, then added, "See there, the two of you have something in common after all."

"What's this about a pedestal?" Alison asked.

Rosalie's eyebrows lifted. "Haven't you been watching TV?"

"Our things won't be arriving for another day or so."

"Haven't you seen the paper?"

"I haven't subscribed yet."

"What about the radio?"

"The only one I have is in the car and there's something wrong with it."

"Mercy me," the older woman said, touching a plump cheek. "If you're going to live in Oklahoma, you've got to have a radio, preferably one that runs on batteries. You know that *Oklahoma!* song about "when the wind comes sweeping down the plains"?

Alison nodded absently.

"Well, it also comes a-twistin'. We're right at the start of tornado season. It peaks in May. You've got to be ready to head for the basement when the siren goes off."

Alison looked at her warily. "Does that happen a lot?"

"Yep. They could strike at any time. Logan County is smack in the middle of tornado alley."

Alison bit a thumbnail.

"Now, don't you worry. Cimarron's still here, isn't

it? Been here since 1889. Of course, you never know. Let's see, where was I?"

"You left Stefan standing on his pedestal."

"That's right." She took a quick sip of coffee. "It happened like this: The newborn daughter of some business tycoon in Oklahoma City was kidnapped right out of the hospital. She was just a few hours old. They brought in the FBI, since kidnapping is a federal crime, you know. After the kidnappers made contact with the family, asking for one million dollars' ransom, they somehow traced their location to an abandoned farm house. They started a-shootin' and while the kidnappers were trying to save their hides, Stefan crawled in through a back window and got the baby. They fired a few shots at him when they realized what had happened, but luckily, they missed. It was even on TV."

Alison sat in silence, feeling somewhat chastened. "I guess a man who braves a hail of gunfire to rescue a baby can't be all bad."

Rosalie shook her head. "Now, what gave you such a bad impression of him?"

Alison told her about the mixed-up marriage proposal.

"Oh, good heavens," Rosalie said with a burst of laughter.

"Make him the patron saint of kidnapped babies, but I don't want to deal with him anymore," Alison said, massaging her forehead. "He gives me a headache."

"That's better than a heartache. He's broken a few, I hear."

Alison's gaze locked on to hers.

"And if you want to avoid him, you'll have to work pretty hard at it," Rosalie continued. "He lives just down the street."

Alison's stomach tightened. "He failed to mention that."

"Actually, he's gone most of the time, working on one case or another, but he has an apartment on the top floor of the Yale Hotel. It's been in the family for several generations. He's usually there on weekends. He was very sweet about coming to visit his aunt Lura Bea."

"That's nice," Alison said blandly.

Rosalie patted Alison's hand, then stood up. "I'm so pleased you bought the house. I know it's going to be lovely when you finish it. I'm going to leave and let you get back to work."

"Rosalie, about the house," Alison said. "I'm really sort of embarrassed to bring it up because it seems so silly, but . . ." She looked over her shoulder to make sure Alex wasn't within earshot. The boys were still in the kitchen, trying to impress each other with how high they could count. "Do you think there was anything to Lura Bea's suspicions that the house was haunted?" she whispered.

Rosalie sat down. Wrinkles formed in her brow. "I hardly think so, but nobody was ever able to talk her out of it."

"But she was very old and perhaps forgetful."

Rosalie nodded. "In her last year, she'd lost her edge, all right. But Lura Bea had been claiming for decades that the house had some sort of, well . . . She called it a 'presence.' "

Alison shifted uneasily in her chair. "I really don't believe in ghosts. But just the same, maybe if I'd known, I would have thought twice about buying the house."

Rosalie's eyes narrowed. "You didn't know?"

She shook her head slowly.

"Lura Bea's stories have made this house into something of a local legend," Rosalie said. "Parents have passed on stories to their children, and the children have put new twists on them. Of course, everyone knows that it's probably fiction, but that doesn't stop that kind of talk from going around."

Alison experienced a sinking feeling.

"I think it's nonsense myself," she went on. "And as much as I loved Lura Bea, I have to admit she was eccentric. The old dear lived in the past. She just wasn't of this century, even though she was born in it. Although there's never been any evidence other than her word that the house is haunted, people just assume it is. I think it was why none of the locals wanted to buy it. It was on the market for quite a while."

Alison's spirits sank like an elevator going down another floor.

Rosalie patted her hand. "Don't let that bother you. It's a beautiful house, a real bargain. Once you fix it up and let in some sunlight, the silly stories will stop. After all, you're young and energetic and you have that sweet little boy. You're hardly the type of person people associate with a haunted house."

Rosalie's reassurances, however, seemed to sail right over Alison's head and out the smudged dining room windows. Silly stories or not, people believed them. Haunted or not, it was enough that the house had frightened one little boy.

On Saturday morning, Alison found it was getting harder to summon energy from her dwindling reserves. The more she worked, the bigger the job grew. The wallpaper had been stripped from the parlor, only to expose large expanses of crumbling plaster that had to be patched. A scraper had slipped and she'd managed to crack a window. And all but the broken one had been painted shut. Beyond the parlor lay seven other rooms, not counting bathrooms.

Alison was alone in the house for the first time since her arrival. Alex had been invited next door to play with Mikey. Outfitted in old, black leggings, an over-sized gray sweatshirt with frayed cuffs, and red sneakers with a hole in one toe, she stood in the parlor. She was consulting the plaster chapter of one of the how-to books she'd brought with her, when she was interrupted by a rapping on the front door.

She pulled it open to find Stefan Yale standing on the porch as if he had every right to be there. She felt a quick tightening in her chest.

"You're overjoyed to see me, I see." His eyes glistened. "But you can hold off clicking your heels together until I get your new doorbell installed."

"Doorbell? But I didn't ask for one."

"I saved you the trouble," he said, holding up a brown striped bag marked "Murphy's Hardware."

Alison gave him a grudging look. He wore a faded plaid flannel shirt, jeans that fit snugly over long, lean legs, and hiking boots that appeared to have actually been hiked in. Next to his feet sat what appeared to be a small toolbox.

"The catch is that you have to let me in first," he said, looking at her expectantly. A few errant strands of black hair grazed his brow. "I hope you will, because I'm really here to make amends."

Alison awkwardly moved aside. He picked up the toolbox and stepped over the threshold in one powerful stride.

"Shouldn't you be out rescuing babies or something?" she asked.

Ignoring her, he opened the bag and pulled out a box illustrated with doorbell components. "Did you know that some doorbells actually play songs?" he asked casually. "With me as your guest, I figured you might be thinking along the lines of Michael Jackson's "Beat It."

Alison smiled—barely.

"You know, you could light up this whole place with your smile, if you just would," he said, unscrewing the old chime box near the top of the door. He hardly needed a ladder.

Alison felt her coloring deepen. He was a ladies' man all right, and she wasn't going to play his game.

"You never said what tune you selected," she said, changing the subject on purpose.

"The decision was too agonizing," he said, turning toward her. "Instead, I got a simple, harmless chime. I haven't heard it, but I imagine it sounds something like 'Avon calling.' "

"I could live with that."

He removed the outer covering of the mechanism, set it on the floor, and brushed his hands together. "Excuse me while I go out and shut the power off. Forgetting that little trick can give a man an unhealthy glow."

He strode through the kitchen and out the back door, leaving Alison slightly dazed. The room seemed to fall in on itself in his absence. The light in the ancient fixture in the parlor ceiling turned dark, adding to the dramatic effect of his departure. His annoying flippancy aside, he was almost companionable. That he could have such an effect on her left her suddenly feeling vulnerable, something she could hardly afford when her future and that of her son seemed to be resting on a teetering old house.

A moment later, he reappeared.

"You certainly seem to know your way around the place," Alison said.

"I know every nook, cranny, and crack."

"Crack?" Alison repeated hoarsely.

He took a screwdriver out of the toolbox and gave it an expert flip. "When I was a boy, I liked to come over and play. I hid in the closets and slid down the banister."

"What's that about a crack?" she repeated impatiently.

He exposed two menacing-looking wires, their copper tentacles reaching out in opposite directions. "This wiring belongs in a museum," he muttered absently.

Alison frowned, placing her hands on her hips. "Do I have to rob a bank to get your attention? What were you saying about a crack?"

He turned quickly and faced her, his mouth in a slight frown. "Just a new twist on an old expression, although I imagine there are plenty of cracks around."

Her insides stirred uneasily. "They're not in the foundation, I hope. The inspection report said there weren't any cracks beyond normal settling." She strode over to the worst wall, where the jagged fissure went from ceiling to floor like a lightning bolt. "This doesn't look like normal settling to me."

Stefan laid down his screwdriver and walked over to inspect. He stroked the crease in his chin. His expression was pinched. "Hmmm. I never noticed this before."

"That's because it was covered up with about four layers of wallpaper," she said contentiously.

He ran a hand through his thick hair. "Well, it wouldn't hurt to take a look at the foundation."

She breathed in sharply and followed him outside, her heart tripping with dread. Stefan knelt and pulled some ivy away from the sandstone blocks that supported the house, exposing a raw crack about a quarter of an inch wide.

"Good grief!" Alison gasped, throwing her hands over her mouth. "This place is falling down."

"Not by a longshot," he countered, poking at the crevice with a finger. "A little settling, maybe, but it looks worse than it is because there's some mortar missing. Probably all it needs is a little patching."

She looked at him warily. "What do you mean 'probably'?"

Stefan stood up and put his arm around her shoulder. "I mean that you shouldn't worry."

The heat of his fingers burned through the fleece of her sweatshirt. "How could I not worry?" she asked, stepping out of his grasp and facing him squarely. "I'm the new owner of a house that has charms that seem to be entirely superficial. Yesterday, I found out that practically everyone in town believes it's haunted and when it was for sale, nobody but me would touch it with a ten-foot pole. Today, I learn that it's cracking in two."

He took her firmly by the elbow and led her to the porch swing. He sat next to her, draping an arm over the back. His fingers brushed the nape of her neck, sending an uneasy stirring through her. "Who told you that everyone thinks the house is haunted?" he asked softly.

"Rosalie from next door."

His chin crinkled. "I think it would be more accurate to say that everyone would like to think so. They're being silly, Alison."

"Would you think it was silly if I told you that Alex

awoke in the middle of the night, saying he heard footsteps?"

"Yes," he said without even blinking. "Suggest something imaginary to a child and he'll turn it into reality."

"But I never told him, never even suggested it," she countered.

He turned to face her, the corner of his mouth tucked into a look that was clearly chiding. "I thought you told me you don't believe in ghosts."

"I don't, but—"

"Then case closed," he said.

Alison took a deep breath and got up. "Then I guess you should go back to my antique wiring and I should go back to my cracked walls."

He cocked his head, the lights in his eyes dancing playfully as he studied her for a moment. She marched impatiently into the house, and he followed.

As Stefan replaced the bell, Alison popped open a can of spackling compound and started to work on the cracks. She started near the ceiling where the big, diagonal fissure began. Poised on a ladder, she sneaked a look at Stefan, who was working happily, singing some silly song about Johnny Yuma, a rebel who roamed through the West. His rich baritone voice was surprisingly well-pitched. From above, his shoulders looked particularly broad and square, his hair as dark and glossy as a raven's wing. That was another annoying aspect of Stefan Yale. Too much attractiveness was wasted on him.

Well, he could afford to be in an aggravatingly

cheerful mood. It wasn't his house. She was hating him for it, craning her neck to get a better look at the object of her derision, when she accidentally smacked her head against the ceiling. She felt a dull pain, followed by several sharp taps on the head and a shower of dust and old plaster.

Coughing, she fumbled blindly down the ladder. Suddenly she felt Stefan's hands around her waist, lifting her down.

"Are you all right?" he asked, brushing the bits of plaster from her hair.

She nodded numbly, too surprised to speak.

He lifted her chin with one finger and gently wiped the dust away from her face with his other hand. Alison looked up to avoid his pale gaze. Above her head was a large patch of exposed lath.

"I'd like to know which of Lura Bea's heirs managed to unload this house on me," she grumbled.

A muscle in his jaw twitched. "I'm afraid I'm the one."

Chapter Three

"You?" she choked. "How could you?" Her voice had a tendency to fail her when she was angry. With the back of a shaky hand, she brushed away a granule of plaster that had caught at the corner of her mouth. Her eyes locked on his, she took a step toward him.

He held his ground. "It's a perfectly good house, ideal for a bed and breakfast. You evidently thought so yourself."

Alison picked a fragment of plaster out of her hair and tossed it at his chest. As he looked down at her, his perfectly sculpted mouth twitched with amusement.

"It's a wreck and you knew it," she said, further enraged. "It's probably haunted and you knew it. What else do you know that you're not telling me?"

The cool gray in his eyes heated to a smoky color. "There's nothing, Alison. You have to expect certain problems with a one-hundred-year-old house." His voice was smooth, and entirely too unaffected.

She sucked in a breath of indignation. "That sleazy little real estate man you hired, that Mr. Coury, bragged about the inspector. No wonder. He was probably one of his cronies."

He hadn't moved an inch and neither had she. There was barely enough room to pass a basketball between them. Alison stared at him, disturbingly aware of how little space they shared. He smelled of freshly laundered flannel and something faintly evergreen. And for the first time, she noticed a small white scar on his chin.

She blinked first. With her heart racing, she moved back a half step, her head remaining at a stubborn angle.

"Come to think of it, your absence at the signing of the contract was rather conspicuous," she said, surveying him with narrowed eyes.

"I was out of town working a case," he said dispassionately.

"That's a nice, tidy excuse. What about the other heirs?"

"They had an even better one."

"What's that?" she asked warily.

"They're dead."

A gap of silence followed. "You're it? You're all there is?"

Stefan nodded slowly. Her eyes dropped to the scar on his chin.

"Aside from Coury, I'm all there is to blame, that is if you insist on holding yourself blameless," he said.

She swallowed hard. He didn't need to say what he was really thinking. "Rosalie said the house was on the market for a long time because of the ghost stories. *That* wasn't mentioned on the disclosure form."

He took her firmly by the shoulders, his eyes alight with intensity. "Alison, there *are* no ghosts. There are no boxes to check on a real estate form to indicate whether or not a house is haunted. As Lura Bea's sole heir, I signed everything in good faith. There's not a thing wrong with this house that can't be fixed. There's not an occurrence in it that can't be explained."

He released her as suddenly as he'd seized her and turned away, accidentally catching the toe of one of his boots on a box in a corner in the parlor. The box along with a broken tricycle, an ancient vacuum cleaner and the other things that Alison hadn't quite known what to do with had remained there.

He surveyed the mess with a frown, then ran a hand through his hair. "You needn't have carried all this down from the attic closet by yourself."

Alison's lips parted in surprise. "I didn't. It was sitting in the floor when I came."

Stefan responded with a sidelong look of skepticism.

"Honest," she said, holding up two plaster-dusted hands. "I didn't touch it."

He studied her with bemused wariness. "You're

good. Have you ever thought about auditioning for the theater? You might get me to believe in ghosts after all."

"I'm not putting you on. My stage career ended when my tutu fell down during a dance recital."

He smiled crookedly, his gaze shifting to her Spandex-covered ankles. "I wish I'd been there."

She shot him a look of disgust.

"Back to what you were saying," he continued, giving the tricycle a slight push with his foot. "It was a good attempt at a ghost story, but it won't work—at least not with me."

Alison sighed in frustration. "I'm not making this up."

His mouth tightened into a straight line. "Well, let's pretend that you're not. There's a logical explanation for these things being here."

She stared at him for a moment. "Who else could have moved those things? Did anyone else have a key to the house?"

"The real estate people. So there," he said with a tone of satisfaction. "Let's get back to work."

"But why would they move them?" she contested.

"Lots of reasons."

"You certainly are assuming for a professional investigator."

He suddenly looked tired. "If you so much as hint once more that this house might be haunted, you're going to see a grown man cry."

Without saying another word, he strode back to the

door with a purposeful gait, picked up his screwdriver, and resumed work on the doorbell. He seemed to be putting so much torque into the effort that Alison was afraid he'd strip the threads right off the screws.

Chastened, she returned to the cracks in the plaster, using a putty knife to fill them in with spackling compound. A tense silence hung over the parlor, broken only by a rattle here and a scrape there. She sneaked a glance at him out of the corner of her eye. He was sticking his screwdriver in his snug back pocket.

"Why did you decide to sell the house?" she ventured.

He turned, his mouth contorted slightly in thought. "Memories," he said finally.

"What sort of memories?"

His footsteps echoed in the nearly empty room as he came toward her. He leaned against the piano. "This is where the family congregated on holidays. There weren't many of us—I was the only child—but it had sort of a *Little House on the Prairie* air about it.

"Aunt Lura Bea was a great believer in family and tradition. She was rooted here. Her parents came here in a covered wagon and staked a claim during the Land Run of 1889, the first time this land was officially opened to settlers. The town of Cimarron sprang up overnight and so did the opportunities. Her father started Cimarron's first newspaper and they stayed.

"This house was a wedding gift from her father. It represents family history. But for me, it also represents something I plan to stay away from."

Alison bit her bottom lip "You're not talking about

termites and other problems of home ownership, are you?"

He folded his arms across his broad chest and scolded her with his eyes. "I'm talking about marriage and family."

His gaze was so direct and clear, so laden with unwavering determination, that she blinked.

"Let's get back to work," he said suddenly, his voice tight. He turned toward the door. This time, he went outside, giving her the sensation of a large truck having passed her at high speed.

Alison fumbled with the spackle, unsure where she left off, accidentally dropping some on her foot. When it came to marriage, this was a man with his mind made up, locked up, and the key thrown away. Not that it made any difference to her, of course.

A few moments later, the light over Alison's head blinked on. Two nail-hole repairs later, the doorbell rang. It was a two-tone chime, bright and cheerful, like the closing notes of a children's song.

She stepped out on the porch to investigate. Stefan punched the button again. It was surrounded by a pretty, oval brass plate.

"There you are," he said. "The doorbell stands at the ready for guests. What are you going to call this place?"

She hesitated a moment. So far, the man hadn't been terribly encouraging about her bed and breakfast plan. "The Prairie Flower Inn."

"Not bad," he said with a shrug of a square shoulder.

She felt a tiny wave of relief. "Thank you for installing the bell. How much do I owe you?"

"Nothing," he said quickly.

"But it cost something, and you spent time putting it in."

He placed his hands on his lean hips. "I owed it to you."

Baffled, she looked at him. "I don't understand."

"I left you a lot of work to do. Have you ever redone an old house by yourself before?"

She shook her head, loath to admit she hadn't, at least to him. "But I've got books on everything."

He gave her a terse little smile that left her slightly annoyed. "Then I'll leave you to your work," he said with a quick wave.

His exit from the porch was blocked by two small boys. One was Alex, again wearing the black patch and pirate's hat, the other was Mikey, sporting a curled mustache that appeared to be drawn from eyebrow pencil and an earring made from a canning jar lid. It hung from his ear by a loop of green yarn. A red bandanna tied around his head drooped over one eye, and he carried Alex's plastic sword.

"Walk the gangplank!" Alex yelled. "We're pirates!"

Mikey jabbed the sword into Stefan's solar plexus for emphasis, then gave it a little twist.

"Boys!" Alison was not amused.

But Stefan clearly was. He slipped the bandanna off Mikey's head and tied it around his eyes. "Good-bye, cruel world," he said, shuffling toward the edge of the porch with his arms outstretched. He bumped into the porch swing. He bumped into the house. He bumped into the balustrade surrounding the porch as the children giggled. Then he threw himself over the porch railing and landed with a roll. He came to a stop with his face against the ground, the bandanna askew. He lay deathly still, the fresh, green blades of an iris plant rising around his ear.

Laughing, the boys ran around to the side of the porch to claim their prey. Alex gave him a nudge on the shoulder but there was no response. Mikey gave him a push. Together, they gave him a push and a nudge, but nothing moved except for a few strands of dark hair ruffled by the wind. Mikey gave him a poke in the spine with the sword, but the man remained as motionless as a boulder.

"Mommy," Alex called, "he won't wake up."

Alison, watching from the porch, skittered down the steps and tore around the house to where Stefan lay, her heart kicking. She dropped to a kneeling position over his long body. He was incredibly still. For an instant, all she could do was stare. First a ghost, then a cracked foundation and now what—a man who had fallen and broken his skull on her property? Think of the legal consequences. Or what if . . . ? Oh, heavens. He'd gone and killed himself.

Alison placed a trembling hand gently on his back. It was very warm, with very firm muscles that seemed to ripple through the soft flannel of his shirt. She moved her hand to his neck and his pulse jumped under her fingers. It was a good, strong one. She took a deep and gasping breath of relief and homed in on his face. All she could see was part of a jaw with the faint outline of dark beard. Afraid to move him, she stroked his hair, not knowing what else to do. It was thick and smooth, like that of a boy.

"Stefan?" she said, her voice tinged with alarm. Suddenly, in one whirling motion, he rolled over and grabbed her by the shoulders, pulling her face within inches of his. There was a playfully wicked gleam in his eyes.

"Thought I'd been deep-sixed, didn't you?"

She heard the children giggling in the background as she stared at him in indignation. She tried to pull away but he wouldn't let go. His touch sent unwanted prickles marching up and down her spine.

"Do another trick, Uncle Stefan," Mikey begged.

"Yeah, Uncle Stefan," Alex added.

Alison shot up, freeing herself from his grasp. "Trick? And what's this 'uncle' business?" she asked, casting a caustic look at her son.

Stefan stood up and brushed off his clothes. There was mud on one knee and a streak of dirt on one cheek. "Well, you see, Mikey and I go way back, don't we, Mikey?"

The boy gave him an admiring nod, half his eyebrow-pencil mustache now missing.

Stefan picked a piece of straw off his elbow. "Aunt Lura Bea suggested that he give me the honored title of *uncle*. When I'd come to visit her, Mikey would come over and I'd come up with a trick or two to entertain him. One was playing dead. So there you have it, the whole story."

Alison studied him sullenly. "Very funny."

Stefan's mouth twisted into an ironic smile. "You were actually worried that I was really hurt?"

"Yes, I was," she said, leveling a hard gaze at him. "You scared me."

"I'm touched," he said lightly. "I didn't know you cared."

Her bottom lip tightened in exasperation.

He took a half step toward her, his gaze locked tightly on her face. "Did you know that when you're mad those little lights in your eyes take on the shape of daggers?"

Alison threw her head back and looked up at the sky so he couldn't see her eyes at all. "Is there anything you don't notice?"

"Not much gets past me. After all, I'm a trained observer. Want to see my badge? It came out of a box of Crunchy Crisps."

Her eyes snapped back to his. They glistened playfully.

"Don't you ever take anything seriously?" she asked.

"Don't you take anything lightly?" he countered.

She sighed. "I guess I should just be grateful you didn't scare the boys."

Stefan looked down at them with a conspiratorial grin. "We boys stick together, don't we?" He crouched on one knee in front of Alex. "By the way, that's a dandy pirate outfit you've got there. Do you know who it used to belong to?"

Alex shook his head. His eye patch had fallen around his neck.

"It was mine. It was my Halloween costume one year. I think it was the same year that Tommy Witherspoon's father accidentally backed over my sack of treats."

Alex looked mildly alarmed. "You don't want it back, do you?"

"No, I bequeath it to you. It's yours now."

The child's face brightened. "Oh, boy, thanks."

"Why don't you guys run off and play a little more?" He turned toward Alison. "That is, if it's all right with you."

Alison looked at her watch and brushed off the plaster dust. "Alex, lunchtime is in an hour. I'll come and get you."

The boys took off down the sidewalk, running, and she watched until they disappeared behind Rosalie's fence. She turned toward Stefan.

"How did Lura Bea manage to have your Halloween costume?"

"My mother had it, actually. When she died, those things ended up in Lura Bea's attic. A sentimental lot my family was."

"And what about the tricycle?"

"It was my father's."

"You should keep it in a safer place," she admonished.

"I'm afraid I haven't given it much thought."

Her lips parted in surprise. "Those things are price-less, at least from a sentimental standpoint."

He looked at her without emotion. "Sentimentality is something in which I don't indulge."

She studied him for a moment. His bottom lip had taken on a stubborn line.

"I'll put the tricycle back in the attic, then, where Lura Bea had it," she said. "I refuse to allow history to be put in the dump."

The corner of his mouth quirked upward into a wry smile. "If you want, I've got some vintage running shoes you can have too."

"I'm going back to work," she said tersely, turning on her heel.

He caught her by the elbow. "When was the last time you sat down and read the comics or indulged in something you enjoy? When was the last time you did anything that wasn't connected to scraping, sanding, steaming, or moving? When was the last time you had a little fun?"

"It doesn't matter. I have work to do, a business to start, a child to raise."

"But it does matter, unless you want to be so ex-hausted when your first guests arrive that you fall face-down in their French toast."

She planted her hands on her hips. "You don't have any idea, do you? That figures for a bachelor. Rosalie told me all about you."

Smile lines fanned out from his eyes. "Rosalie doesn't know *all* about me."

"That's a good thing, for her sake."

The crease in his chin deepened. "Let's get back to the topic at hand. Let's talk about what's good for you. I'm going to see that you get several hours of rest and recreation."

"Just how are you going to do that?" she asked, piqued.

"I'm coming over tonight," he said firmly. "I'm bringing supper with me."

"But I have to work on the parlor," she protested.

"Expect me around six." He turned and walked away.

The only concession she'd made to his impending visit was to take a shower and shampoo the dust out of her hair. She blew it dry into its usual tousled style. She put on a pair of clean but faded jeans, loafers, and a red turtleneck, foregoing any make-up except a little mascara and lip gloss. She was certain Stefan Yale was used to having women dress up for him. Well, she wasn't one going to.

She was using every spare moment to finish patching one of the parlor walls when the new doorbell chimed melodically. Her neatnik son, who had been painstakingly arranging toy building blocks on the dining room table, jumped down from his chair and ran toward the door, his bangs flying.

"Uncle Stefan!" he cried.

Alison winced. Alex was becoming too familiar with this man, too soon. Never might be too soon when it came to Stefan Yale.

She opened the door and he stood near the threshold, practically filling the door frame. His hair glistened from a light mist that had started to fall and he was holding the largest pizza box Alison had ever seen.

Alex, outfitted in his customary overalls, romped up to Stefan and hooked him around the knee before he could get in the house.

"There's my good buddy," Stefan said, tousling his hair. Then he looked up and his eyes caught hers, causing her stomach to tighten. "And there's my not-so-good buddy," he added, his gaze lingering mischievously on her. "I hope you hate anchovies," he said, handing her the box.

She looked at him suspiciously. "You loaded up on purpose, hoping I would, right?"

He pried Alex off his leg and stepped inside. "No, I left them off. I hate anchovies."

"I hate ant chovies too," Alex said, seemingly eager to agree with Stefan.

"You don't even know what they are," Alison said, setting the box on the dining room table.

"Yes, I do," he insisted. "It's something that belongs to an ant."

Alison's gaze caught Stefan's and they laughed together. His smile was broad and white; his eyes bright, yet with a dusky hint of intimacy. It was the sort of moment she and Kevin had shared. The realization that she was sharing it with someone like Stefan Yale led her to look awkwardly away. "Thank you for the pizza," she said, somewhat stiffly. "You really didn't have to."

"I know," he said, "but I wanted to."

The pizza was otherwise laden with every customary topping. Alison served it on a red-and-white checked tablecloth and blue and white Currier and Ives plates she'd brought from Texas. Alex asked questions between bites. "What are those red things in the olives? How do they get in there?"

For a man who was single and determined to stay that way, Stefan didn't seem to tire of Alex's questions. He answered them with patience and good humor. In way, Alison was glad his attention was partially focused on the child. His strong presence was something she'd been trying all evening to minimize. But she couldn't help but notice how the light from the chandelier brought out the touches of silver in his hair and cast a glow over the finely chiseled lines of his face. For an instant, she almost forgot that he'd unloaded a house on her that no one else seemed to want to touch. And while she was not entirely charmed, Alex clearly was.

After a dessert of vanilla ice cream, which Alison served in little stemmed glasses, Stefan suggested some after-dinner piano music.

"Are you going to play the piano?" Alex asked. Alison reached over with a napkin and removed a smudge of pizza sauce from his cheek.

"No, my boy," Stefan said. "You are."

The boy tilted his head. A puzzled expression came over his face. "But I don't know how."

"Come on, both of you," he said, getting up.

They went into the parlor where Stefan carefully

rolled back the heavy plastic drop cloth that Alison had placed over the piano. Under that was a padded cover which he also lifted, revealing a gleaming black instrument, its keys yellowed with age.

"Aunt Lura Bea must have given a million lessons on this," he said. "I was probably the most resistant of all her students because I had to give up sports one day a week. At the time, I thought that was one day too many. A silly boy I was."

With the ease of a tennis player tossing up a ball, Stefan lifted Alex and put him on the bench. He sat beside him. "Here's a little song that goes this way." He touched his fingers to the keyboard. " 'This is up. This is down. This is up and down,' " he sang. "Now, you try it. I'll help you."

He placed the boy's small fingers on the keyboard and guided them through the three-note tune. Alex turned to his mother with such a look of surprised delight that the old parlor might as well have been Carnegie Hall. Her heart gave a thump.

He played it again with Stefan's assistance, then by himself, over and over until he began to lean into his shoulder.

"I think it's time for bed, maestro," she said. "You can play some more tomorrow."

His face crumpled in disappointment. "But I want to stay up."

"Tell you what, pal," Stefan said. "I'll play you a song while you go to sleep and we'll do this again some other time."

Hesitantly, Alex let her take him to bed. They were

barely at the top of the stairs when Alison heard the strains of a familiar Chopin prelude, the notes rich and played with feeling. The warm tones spiraled slowly upward like curls of smoke. She was so surprised by such an expert execution of the piece that she stopped for a moment. It seemed oddly incongruous that the man at the keyboard was also a man who carried a gun.

After getting Alex tucked in, she sat at the edge of his bed, stroking his hair softly and listening to the strains of the music. As his eyes closed, she studied the soft contours of his face and felt a mixture of hope and concern. He'd adapted to the move better than she'd imagined and he'd quickly made new friends. But there was something about his quick attachment to Stefan Yale that left her unsettled.

When his breathing took on the slow rhythm of sleep, she quietly left his bedside. By the time she closed the door behind her and started down the stairs, the music had changed. It was another prelude, a little softer, a little slower, but still played with the same intensity of emotion.

He looked up when she entered the parlor and his fingers went still on the keyboard.

"Very nice," she said. "Is there anything you can't do?"

He turned toward her, resting his hands on his thighs. They were large and square with long fingers that looked both sensitive and powerful. "I can't whistle."

She touched the gleaming black instrument. "Why

would someone who plays so beautifully want to sell the piano on which he learned?"

"You ask a lot of questions, know that?" His gaze moved playfully over her face.

"Why would you want to let it go with the house?" she persisted.

"It's just a piano," he said, clamping down the keyboard cover. He began to unfold the quilted pad that covered the instrument. "There are thousands like it. When I found out that this was going to be a bed and breakfast, it seemed appropriate to leave it. Guests like that sort of thing—better than my neighbors at the hotel would."

Alison studied his handsome face. There was a stiffness in his jaw that she hadn't noticed before. He hurriedly finished covering the piano and turned away from it. Didn't the man have a sentimental bone in his body?

"You'll be having senior citizens standing around it, singing 'Good Night, Irene,' " he continued. "I think Aunt Lura Bea would have been delighted with that. Any more questions?"

Alison, mildly dissatisfied with his response, shook her head anyway. He took a few paces over the scuffed parlor floor. Alison couldn't help but notice the power in his bearing. He picked up the pirate's hat that Alex had left on an old chair and smiled slightly.

"Alex can ask some real mind-benders." He set the hat down and strolled back toward her.

"You get the easy questions," she said. "I get the hard ones—like why is his father never coming back."

Stefan's gaze snapped to hers. His expression turned somber. "How long has it been?

Alison swallowed hard. "Two years. He was a military pilot, a hopeless daredevil. Not even Alex's birth could ground him. Something went wrong during an air show and there was a crash."

Stefan's face went rigid. "I'm sorry."

She managed a tight smile. "Thank you, but I'm all right, now. We both are, all things considered. All I want now is to raise Alex in a reasonably secure setting, to get the bed and breakfast established, and to put down some roots."

His gaze shifted downward as if he were having some sort of troublesome thought.

"Is something wrong?" she asked softly.

He looked up, his mouth tightening into a strained smile. He reached out, grabbed a tendril of her hair, and gave it a playful tweak. "Nothing that should ever worry you."

She looked at him, puzzled.

"Good night," he said quickly, his eyes murky.

And almost as spontaneously as he'd invited himself over, he was gone, leaving her feeling strangely empty inside. He was too attractive, too funny and too good with children, as if he hadn't already given her enough to worry about.

Chapter Four

Murphy's Hardware sat squeezed between an antiques store and a veterinary clinic on a brick street that ran neatly through Cimarron's Victorian-styled downtown area. It smelled of new metal and old wood and of a half century gone by.

Alison thumbed through sample books of wallpapers. She envisioned the parlor in stripes with a border running just under the crown molding. But there were too many choices. There were narrow stripes and wide stripes and stripes of all colors. Dizzily, she turned back and forth through the pages. And the borders? It was too hard to know which one would be just right. She ruminated on this while keeping an eye on Alex. At the moment, he was a few paces away watching a clerk stock a glass case with drill bits and other gadgets. Just minutes ago, she'd had to reel him in by an overall strap when he tried to tag along with a couple of old men who were looking for fishing lures.

Reluctantly, she'd come to realize that Alex needed a significant male figure in his life. As soon as the house was finished and the tourist season was over, they would go visit her brother, David.

A year after Kevin's death, she had reluctantly accepted a dinner invitation from a very nice man. He was an accountant with a safe, predictable and orderly life. But by the time the cherries jubilee had arrived, she knew that she'd made a mistake, that it was too early for her to be thinking of someone else. The hole in her heart was just too big to gamble on something as risky as love. Loving someone meant the possibility of losing them.

And that brought her to what was really wreaking havoc with her concentration. It wasn't the infinity of wallpaper choices or Alex, who at the moment was meticulously building a barn out of some paint stirring sticks a clerk had given him. It was Stefan Yale—the crooked smile, the powerful shoulders, the strong gait. Somewhere between the Sarasota stripes and the Chesapeake stripes the awful realization hit: What she was feeling was a tug of physical attraction. She closed the sample book with such a snap that it caused the people around her to turn in her direction.

Her cheeks warming slightly, she wandered over to the paint samples. Stressful life changes, such as a move, were bound to produce some irrational thoughts. And she was tired, having worked from early morning to midnight since she'd arrived. Why was she thinking about an avowed bachelor who thrived on danger? She massaged her forehead to ease the beginning pangs of a headache. She had to start getting more rest. She needed to get Stefan Yale out of her life.

Collecting her wits and Alex, Alison bought two gallons of off-white enamel for the woodwork, a fistful of foam rubber brushes, a half dozen drop cloths, rubber gloves and a packet of sandpaper. She checked out three wallpaper sample books.

She parceled out the lighter objects for Alex to carry to the minivan, which was parked a half block down from the hardware store. She followed, lugging a half gallon of paint in each hand and holding a paint stick between her teeth.

"I'll help with those," a familiar voice said.

The stick fell from her mouth and clattered to the sidewalk. She spun around to find Stefan a few paces behind her. He was suited in his usual, somber charcoal gray. Although it was past the end of the work day, not a thread or a hair seemed out of place.

"Uncle Stefan!" Alex dropped the bag he was carrying and flung himself in his direction.

"Hey, Alex," he greeted, placing his hand briefly on the boy's shoulder. "How's my top man in Cimarron?"

"Fine," he said, his round, blue eyes shining.

Stefan's gray gaze shifted to Alison, sending her heart over a big bump. "Where did you come from?" she asked.

He reached for both cans of paint, unavoidably touching her hands and sending her pulse skipping. "You know, I asked that same question of my mother once. If I recall, the answer had something to do with a cabbage patch."

Alison cast him a look of impatience. "She would know."

His mouth twitched slightly. "Where would you like me to put these?"

Alison opened up the rear door of the minivan. "Here would be fine."

Seemingly effortlessly, he set the cans down among a few stray toys, including a plastic ball and bat. Copying Stefan's motions, Alex set down his bag of brushes next to the paint.

"Thank you. We can get the rest," Alison said.

Stefan turned toward the sidewalk where they had left the remaining pile of supplies. Ignoring her, he picked up what was left, including the bulky sample books and deftly placed them in the back. "Anything else?" He squinted down at her through a few spikes of dark hair that had fallen over his brow. He looked like Gallahad in gray flannel, strong, capable and ready. Alison was trying her hardest not to notice. So much for her plans to keep him at a distance.

"No, that should do it," she said. She strapped Alex into the backseat and closed the door. "We really should be going, but thank you anyway."

A playful light danced in his eyes. "What's the hurry? Afraid your paint brushes will melt?"

"Go ahead. Amuse yourself." She hurriedly unlocked the door on the driver's side.

With a tight-lipped smile, he shoved his hands into

his pockets and caught up with her in one long stride. "Don't run off just yet. I have some news for you."

Her gaze locked on his.

"The mystery of the wandering junk has been solved. I ran into our mutual acquaintance, Mr. Coury the real estate agent, and he sends his apologies. He had the attic closet cleared out before you looked at the house. The stuff was in the garage, but it was moved to the parlor while the inside of the garage was being treated for termites."

Alison's mouth went dry. "Termites?"

"Don't worry. There weren't any. It's just an inspection and preventative treatment. Aunt Lura Bea had the termite people come once a year, just to be safe. And there's no ghost either, let me repeat."

Alison folded her arms across her chest as if daring him to again make light of her past concerns.

"And another thing," he said. "While you're here, why don't you come up to my apartment for a moment? I'd like to show you something."

Having heard about his ways with women, his apartment was the last place she needed to be. "Thanks, but perhaps some other time." She made a mental note to mark her calendar for never. "It's getting late."

"Forget about your proper little work ethic just for a moment." He slid open the minivan's side door and bent his tall frame to take a look at the boy inside. "Help me convince your mother to come in just for a moment. There's something I'd like to give you."

Alison aimed a laser-like glare at Stefan, but to no avail.

The boy's eyes brightened. "Oh, boy, Mom. Can we go?"

The collar of Alison's denim shirt turned steamy as Stefan's eyes flickered with triumph. He'd gotten her at her weakest point. "All right." She got out and helped Alex out of his seat belt. "A second, maybe."

The boy scrambled out of the car and went skipping onto the sidewalk.

"This way, partner," Stefan said, pointing him toward the end of the block.

Avoiding Stefan's eyes, Alison took Alex's hand. Just wait until she got alone with the man. She'd teach him not to commandeer her son.

"My apartment has a very nice view," Stefan said after a half block of silence. "In fact, I'd just gotten home from work and was standing at the window when I saw you and Alex straggle out of the hardware store. I thought you wouldn't mind a little help." His chin had a crinkle in it that suggested contriteness.

"We weren't straggling."

"All right, a bit of hyperbole, maybe."

"What's purply?" Alex interjected. "I don't like purple."

Despite herself, Alison smiled, then glanced up at Stefan.

He smiled back. Then he stopped, took her by the shoulders, and drew his face closer to hers as if he were examining a set of fingerprints. Her blood warmed as the distance between them narrowed alarmingly. "What's that on your face?" he teased. "Could it really be a smile?"

Rattled by the intimacy of the gesture, she felt her smile dissolve like sugar in water.

"The Alison Perry smile, a rare sighting indeed," he said, seemingly unaffected. His hands dropped from her shoulders as casually as he'd placed them there.

This was a man who handled women with ease, it was clear. A touch on the shoulder, a tug on a tendril of hair. He'd done it a million times.

He stopped in front of a four-story red brick building positioned on a corner. The entrance was covered by a massive green-and-white striped awning. Two small evergreen trees in clay pots flanked the front door. "This is it," he said. "This is home."

Alex looked toward the sky. "You sure have a big house." Although he was of average height for a four year old, he suddenly looked very small next to Stefan's long form.

Stefan laughed softly. "Just a few rooms are mine," he said. "The rest belong to other people."

"What other people?" Alex asked.

"Oh, there's Mr. Pennypacker, retired from the railroad. And there's Collette, rather Miss Carey, kindergarten teacher and part-time model. Very nice neighbors."

The part-time model, in particular, Alison thought dryly.

"And, of course, there are rooms for tourists too. Let's go inside."

He led them to an elevator with gleaming brass trim

and a folding, lattice-like door. He secured it, then hoisted Alex up so he could push the fourth-floor button. A few moments later, the car stopped with a bump.

As they followed Stefan down a hallway carpeted with a dark blue Persian-style runner, Alison tried to wake up from what must surely have been a wayward little daydream. But when Stefan stopped in front of a door at the end of the hall and turned the lock with a loud click, she knew her presence here was all too real.

Stefan might have called it home, but the apartment looked more like what it was—a hotel room. With its basic blue sofa and matching chair, the obligatory end table and lamp, and hotel-issue landscape print on the wall, it could have belonged to anyone. Other than a few scattered newspapers, a briefcase, and a stack of tattered manila folders on the coffee table, there was nothing in the room that said much about the occupant. If anything, it was the absence of personal objects that spoke loudest. Alison scanned the room for photographs or other mementos, but there was nothing. It was the place of a man who didn't intend to put down roots.

Alison tried, but failed to stifle a sneeze.

"Sorry, dusting is not one of my strong suits, but come see the view. That's what I wanted to show you."

Stefan strode over to a set of glass-paneled double doors, perhaps the room's loveliest feature, and reached up to release a latch at the top. When he did, his jacket swung back, briefly exposing the service revolver secured at his waist. Alison's gut clenched. Instinctively, she placed a protective hand on Alex's shoulder, not because she was afraid for him, but because she was afraid for Stefan. The gun represented danger and for her, danger meant loss.

The doors, guarded by a low iron railing, opened onto downtown Cimarron and the vista below. The trees, sprinkled with the barest and tenderest of early spring green, left a number of nearby houses unobscured. One of them was the Prairie Flower Inn, its single, gray-shingled turret pointing toward a gauze of low clouds.

"There's our house," Alison marveled. She held Alex up to see. At a distance, only its charms were visible, its flaws undetectable. Seeing it in a rosy wash of evening light sent a surge of renewed energy through her. "It looks like a doll house."

"I thought you'd enjoy seeing it from a different perspective," Stefan said. "Now, will you forgive me dragging you up here?"

"No." She said it with a smile.

Stefan secured the doors again, then turned to Alex. "And I've got something for you, pal." He disappeared into another room and came back with a large cardboard box under his arm. He knelt down and unsealed it. For an instant, the revolver flashed into view again, causing Alison's stomach muscles to tighten.

He lifted wadded newspaper from the box and pulled out the scuffed engine of a toy train. Alison could tell from the patina that it was not only old but valuable.

"What do you think?" he asked Alex.

"Wow!" he exclaimed, his eyes wide.

"It's yours," he said simply.

Alison's breath caught. "Stefan . . ." Her tone was filled with caution. "Don't tell me you're giving away some heirloom."

"It's a train, that's all," he said without emotion.

Alison looked at him uncomprehendingly.

"Look, Mom," Alex said excitedly, holding up the caboose. With the other hand, he gave Stefan's suit jacket a tug. "Let's play."

"I'm sorry, Alex, but it's time to go home," she interjected. "It's getting dark and supper is on the stove. And Stefan has plans of his own."

The boy's face fell. Stefan cuffed Alex on the shoulder. "Listen. I have an idea. If it's all right with your mother, I'll follow you home and help her unload the things she bought today. Then, I'll help you set up the train. It only takes a few minutes." He cast an inquiring look toward Alison.

She set her jaw sternly. *Ogre,* she thought, fixing her gaze on his. *How am I ever going to get rid of you when you keep playing hero to my son?*

"Shall we go?" he asked, before she could get her wits together. He had the audacity to look amused.

"That seems to already be decided," she said.

He held up his right hand as if he were taking an oath. "I won't stay but a few minutes. Remember, I owe you for unloading a house on you in need of so much work."

She looked at him thoughtfully. He'd outmaneuvered her again.

Little was said during the four-block drive to the Prairie Flower. Alison fought to keep her mind on her driving. She was unaccustomed to having a man in the car, especially one so attractively packaged. In fact, he was an unlikely occupant of a minivan. The man had sleek European import written all over him, the kind meant not so much for family picnics, but for outings with part-time models.

Alison unlocked the oval-paned front door and was immediately struck by the contrast between the old Victorian house and Stefan's spare hotel suite. Despite the disarray of renovation, the cracks and the squeaks, it had the feel of home. The rich aroma of stew wafted from the kitchen, a teddy bear sat on the piano bench, and a framed cross-stitch *Home Sweet Home* sampler that Alison had unpacked sat on the mantel.

Stefan set the cans of paint inside the front door. "Something smells good."

"It's stew," Alex said. "You can stay and have some. "My mom's a real good cooker."

Alison wanted to tape her son's mouth shut. What was he going to do next, invite him to spend the night?

"I bet she does make a mean pot of stew," Stefan responded, his gaze flickering with mischief. "But after I set up your train, I have to be going."

"She makes biscuits with it too. He can have some, can't he, Mom?"

Alison almost wished she hadn't read to him from that children's book about sharing. "Of course," she said, a little too brightly.

"Is that an invitation?" Stefan asked cautiously.

"If you don't mind one that's not engraved."

"And if you clean your plate, you can have a biscuit with lots of honey on it," Alex added.

A smile teased Stefan's lips. "I'd be happy to stay."

"Good," Alison said. Suddenly, she was no longer hungry. "I'll get things ready while you help Alex with the train."

"Can I take Stefan upstairs and show him the fort I built out of blocks?" Alex asked.

"Sure." She turned to Stefan. "He's an architect in the making, always building things, manipulating them until they're perfect."

"Let's go see," Stefan said, his fingers grazing the boy's shoulder. As Alex and Stefan noisily climbed the stairs to the attic, Alison checked the seasoning on the stew. Distracted by Stefan's presence, she burned her tongue. She was going to have to have a talk with Alex about inviting people to dinner without asking her first.

She made the biscuit dough, almost forgetting the baking soda. By the time she got the biscuits rolled out, cut, and into the oven, Stefan and Alex were back downstairs and had the train set up on one end of the long dining room table.

It was a precursor of the electric train. In addition

to the engine, there were six cars of different colors, a track that came together in an oval, and a small station. The station was wood with *Cimarron* lettered on the outside.

Alison stood in the doorway and watched as Stefan gave the engine a nudge and the train went inching around a curve. His collar was unbuttoned and his tie loosened, but the jacket remained on. She suspected, with a sense of gratitude, that it had something to do with the gun.

Alex's mouth formed an *O* of delight as he watched. Stefan straightened, his gaze meeting hers.

"It's hard to tell who is having more fun," she said. "Are you sure you want to give that train up?"

He quickly shook his head. "I'm not a little boy anymore."

No woman could argue with that. "But . . ." Before she could suggest that someday he might change his bachelor ways and have a son of his own, he reached out and flicked her cheek with his thumb.

"Flour," he said, deftly changing the subject.

Her skin tingling where he'd touched her, she turned and went back to the kitchen and absently began stirring the stew. Just what she needed, a certified ladies' man in the house. Why couldn't he go practice his charms somewhere else?

Alex was oblivious to the man's flaws. As they ate, he challenged Stefan to see who could make the best milk mustache. Stefan conceded defeat.

After a dessert of biscuits and honey, Alison told Alex it was bedtime. He took the news with a protest and a pout, but she stood firm. Stefan eased the situation by carrying him upstairs on his shoulders. While Alex took delight in it, Alison found it worrisome. Children made attachments all too easily and Stefan didn't want close connections at all.

After she managed to get Alex into his pajamas and into bed, she returned to the parlor, where Stefan was seated on the old Chippendale sofa. His suit jacket lay over the back. The sleeves of his shirt were rolled up, revealing thick forearms. "You're a good mom," he said. "I know it must be tough raising a child alone."

"I just do the best I can," she said simply. She tried to avoid looking at his waist where she knew the gun would be.

"I'm sure you won't always be raising him alone. The right guy will come along, someone who will be a good father to Alex."

She shrugged and leaned against the piano. "If it happens, fine, but I'm not going out of my way to look for anyone."

"I can't say that I don't look," he said with a roguish glint in his eyes. "I just don't play for keeps."

She stirred uneasily. She had meant what she said about not looking for anyone. Yet, she felt an oddly irrational twinge of disappointment when he'd made it so clear that commitment wasn't for him.

Alison sat on the piano bench to avoid sitting next to him. The light from a Tiffany-style lamp played along his strong jaw and gave his hair the mellow sheen of onyx. He made the room seem smaller and the world more complicated. And for that, she wished he would go home or whatever he called that spare and drab hotel suite.

"Stefan, thank you for the train. It looks like it has been passed down through several generations."

"It was my grandfather's, actually," he said without emotion. "It was passed down to me."

"And you don't want it?" she asked incredulously.

He shook his head adamantly. "No. What good is it to me when Alex can get some enjoyment out of it?"

"But it's a connection to your past, to the people you've loved and who have loved you. Aren't you the least bit sentimental?"

He shook his head.

Alison frowned. "I'll be happy to return it when Alex outgrows it."

"No," he said firmly.

Surprised by the determination in his tone, her gaze lingered on him. "What about the old tricycle and Lura Bea's letters? What about the things from the attic?"

He shrugged. "Sell them to an antiques dealer, give them to the country historical society, throw them out."

She blinked. "It's from your family, Stefan. It has to mean something to you."

He got up, strolled over to the mantel, and picked up the framed *Home Sweet Home* sampler, then set it down. He turned toward her. "Alison, my father was a cop, killed in the line of duty when I was ten years old. My mother was never the same. She died when I was seventeen. The doctor said it was her heart; Lura

Bea said it was grief. Lura Bea took me in because I had nowhere else to go.

"I love my work, Alison. It enables me to help bring about justice in an unjust world, to continue what my father was doing. The bottom line is that I don't want to leave some kid marooned like I was. These things that make you sentimental and nostalgic are simply harsh reminders of how quickly life can change."

Alison felt a sudden chill and slipped her hands inside the opposite sleeves of her sweater. "I understand," she said softly.

He stood up and put on his jacket. "Thanks for a terrific meal. Keep the train."

Before Alison could respond, the patter of footsteps echoed from the top of the stairs. Alex, his face pale and his hair in disarray, ran barefoot toward Alison.

"What are you doing up, Alex?" she asked.

"I heard some more noises."

Chapter Five

Alison grasped Alex's wrists. "What are you talking about?"

"There were noises," he said breathlessly. "Someone knocked my fort down."

Her gaze shot to Stefan.

Stefan showed no reaction. "Take it easy, champ. There couldn't have been anyone upstairs or your mother and I would have heard them. I'm sure there's a logical explanation for this. Stay here and I'll go have a look. I'll be right back." His tone was light.

Alison gave Alex a reassuring hug. "It's nothing. You'll see." She was trying to convince herself as much as him.

"But my fort ... You or Stefan didn't do it, did you?"

A short pause followed. "No." Quickly, she changed the subject. "Let me get you a glass of milk."

The minutes on the clock dragged by as Alison sat

at the kitchen table and waited. A gusty March breeze could have blown the blocks over, but she remembered closing the window just that afternoon. Vibrations could have caused them to topple, but that was unlikely. Alison thought again of Lura Bea's stories and bit down on the crook of her thumb. If the old lady's tales had no credence, where were the sounds of footsteps coming from? Of course, Stefan could be amused. It wasn't this house anymore.

The clatter of footsteps on the bare oak stair treads brought her to her feet. Stefan appeared in the kitchen doorway. His mouth tightened just short of a smile. "I think I've found some evidence of an intruder."

Alison's heart banged against her ribs. "What is it?"

"Come on up," he said calmly. "I'll show you."

"Are you sure it's okay?" she asked, gesturing toward Alex with her eyes.

"I'm sure," he said nonchalantly.

She took the boy's hand and they followed Stefan up the stairs to the third floor where the playroom was located. On the bare oak floor were the remains of the fort that Alex had painstakingly built. All that was left was a crooked foundation and dozens of scattered blocks.

Baffled, Alison studied the mess, then looked at the attic window with its stained-glass border. "The window is locked, just as I left it," she said.

Stefan smiled mysteriously. "Well, just look around some more. It doesn't take a federal agent to figure this one out."

She paced around the ruined fort. "I don't see any-thing."

"Widen your parameters. Keep looking. Keep your eyes to the floor."

She clamped her hands on her hips and looked up at him instead. "Stefan, I want to know what's been scaring Alex and scaring me. I want to know what was scaring Lura Bea. "I want to know now."

Stefan folded his hands over his chest. "Keep look-ing."

Fuming inwardly and not making any effort to dis-guise it, she paced around him. She didn't know if she couldn't see anything or was too mad to see. There was nothing on the scuffed floor but toy blocks. She stopped and took a deep breath. She took a step back-ward, accidentally bumping into a couple of cardboard moving boxes. Suddenly, something dark and crawly and with a long, stringlike tail darted out from between the boxes and scurried past her ankle. She shrieked and leapt backward, accidentally slamming into Ste-fan's chest.

He placed his hands on her shoulders. She felt the low rumble of his laughter in his chest. "It's only a mouse."

Her cheeks turned hot. Not only had mysterious oc-currences been traced to an ordinary mouse, but she realized with no small amount of alarm that she had hurled herself right into Stefan's rock-hard body. Quickly, she pulled away, but her blood continued to race.

"Sorry, I didn't mean . . ."

His eyes shone. "No need to apologize."

"It scared me."

"Not me," Alex said with bravado.

Stefan gave a short laugh. "Well, there you have it. I think your mystery is solved. Fort Apache was felled by a mouse."

Alison was relieved, but she also felt vaguely foolish. "I've never seen one up that close before."

"You may be seeing some more. It's time to set some traps."

"You mean to kill them?"

"Were you thinking of keeping them as pets?"

She wrinkled her nose in distaste.

"That's the best way to put this ghost to rest," he said.

Alison took a deep breath. "You figured all along it was a mouse?"

He nodded. "They leave um . . . clues, calling cards, you might say. Sometimes that includes footprints and chewed and shredded material. That's what I was trying to get you to notice so you could figure it out yourself. Instead, our little friend just boldly presented himself. I was never able to convince Aunt Lura Bea that there are no ghosts here, but I hope that after tonight, I've convinced you."

"I was never convinced there were. It was just that . . ."

"I know. Stories like that die hard."

Alex was realigning Fort Apache's foundation. "Come on, young man," Alison said. "The mystery is solved. It's time to go back to bed."

Alison took him down the half flight of stairs to his room, kissed him on the forehead, and tucked him in.

"Could I say goodnight to Stefan too?" he asked.

Alison turned to find him leaning casually against the doorjamb. He strolled over, bent down, and ruffled the boy's hair. "Good night, buddy."

Suddenly, Alex sat up and threw his arms around Stefan's neck. For an instant, he seemed caught off guard. Awkwardly, his arms folded around the boy's back, sending Alison's heart into a back beat. When Stefan released him, she noticed that his expression was uncharacteristically somber.

All the way down the stairs, the scene stayed in her mind. It was too domestic, too familial, one that shouldn't be repeated. It wouldn't do for Alex to become attached to a man whose idea of hearth and home was probably a stakeout van furnished with binoculars and electronic monitoring equipment.

"Thanks for the supper," he said, stopping at the front door. "I'd forgotten what a home-cooked meal was like."

"Thanks for busting our ghost."

He shrugged. "You might find yourself missing him," he said.

"Not a chance."

They said good night to each other in a stiff and strangely formal way. After Stefan left, Alison stood with her back against the front door. Perhaps there was no ghost, but there was something else: The house seemed very empty without Stefan. That was scary enough in itself.

*   *   *

For the next week, she sanded and scrubbed, stripped and cleaned. She worked every day without stopping, except to cook and to take care of Alex. Once he was in bed, she again picked up her scraper, paint brush, or tool and worked well into the night, until her muscles ached and her limbs grew heavy.

No matter how hard she worked, the renovation project didn't seem to be moving fast enough. There were more layers of wallpaper than she had imagined, more layers of paint, more cracks, and more gaps than she had guessed. Then one night as she sipped a cup of green tea to keep herself awake, she realized with alarm that she was a week behind schedule. According to her very own timetable, the wallpaper was supposed to be up in the parlor and the dining room. It wasn't even up in the parlor. She hadn't yet finished painting the grooved and medallioned woodwork around the windows. But even if she had been ready, the electrician wasn't. The wiring had to be updated before the wallpaper went up, and he'd called to say he was running behind schedule, and he'd be there in a few days.

She hadn't seen Stefan since the mouse was discovered in the attic. That was exactly the way she had wanted it, only she was troubled by the fact that no matter how much she scrubbed and sanded, she couldn't scrub him out of her mind. Every time she remembered the warmth and breadth of his chest and the low rumble of his laughter, she tackled her work with a renewed vengeance.

In the meantime, she managed to catch three mice

in special traps that spared their lives, then she turned them loose in a field. There were no more noises, no more scattered toys. At night, she heard nothing but the hum of the refrigerator.

On Friday morning, Rosalie popped in with Mikey in tow. Alex was at the dining room table with crayons and a coloring book; Alison was painting woodwork.

"I had an idea," Rosalie said. "I know how busy you have been with the house. I was going to take Mikey to the Oklahoma City zoo tomorrow and I was wondering if Alex might like to come along. I read the boys a newspaper story about the new baby elephant and they'd like to see him."

"I don't see why not," Alison said. Both boys began jumping up and down excitedly. "It's really considerate of you to ask. I feel bad that the house is taking up so much of my time."

"Perhaps Alex would like to spend the night at my place too. Mikey is going to stay over and I'm going to pitch a tent in the dining room and maybe roast some hot dogs in the backyard. That would give you a chance to get a little rest."

"What do you think, Alex?" Alison asked.

"Can I?" he asked.

"Of course."

Rosalie patted Alison on the shoulder. "Get some rest, okay, honey? You've been looking awfully tired."

"I'll try," she said, knowing she could scarcely spare the time.

Grateful for Rosalie's support, she put her work aside and made some tea. While the boys were in the kitchen with cookies and milk, they sat at the dining room table.

"Stefan thinks he found our 'ghost.' He discovered mice in the attic," Alison told her.

Rosalie looked at her for a moment without saying anything. "He convinced Lura Bea of that too, but only for a little while."

Alison felt a pang of concern. "What do you mean?"

"She had every exterminator in town go through this house, and she still kept hearing noises."

Alison set down her teacup. "What kind of noises?"

"Squeaks, creaks, footsteps. No one really took her seriously, yet we knew the old dear had hearing like a bat. She had perfect pitch right up to the end. You could hit any note on a piano and she could tell you what it was."

"Old houses do make noises," Alison said. "Wood expands and contracts."

"Exactly. But she insisted she heard footsteps." Her eyes rolled upward.

Alison relaxed slightly. "What about things being moved?"

Rosalie sighed. "She wouldn't back down on that, either. Once she said she left one of her music books on the piano and the next morning, a different book was there—a child's music book. "But you know what?" Rosalie placed a hand over Alison's. "I think she didn't want to let us down. Too many people were having fun with the notion that the house had a ghost."

*   *   *

Alison was all too happy to give up the notion of a ghost. But on Saturday night, while Alex was "camping" next door with Mikey, and she was alone in the old Victorian, her senses went into overdrive. Ordinary noises—from the starts and stops of the refrigerator to the squeak of the rungs of the ladder—took on new and strange qualities. She analyzed every thump, bump, and faucet drip to see if it could be mistaken for something else. She had worked herself into such a heightened sensual state, that when the doorbell rang, she jumped, almost dropping her hammer.

She glanced through the tattered panel of lace covering the front door to find a familiar form shrouded in a wash of light from her bare windows. A feeling of disquiet fluttered through her.

She pulled open the door, the old hinges groaning. Stefan stood with his hands on his hips. His dark hair was pushed haphazardly back from his forehead. Some of it stood in spikes. He wore jeans torn at one knee and a faded flannel shirt with a button missing and the sleeves rolled up. He fidgeted with the energy of a puppy who was anxious to come back inside.

"Oh, it's you," Alison said.

His mouth took on a wry twist. "Who were you expecting, the Dalai Lama?"

"It's almost nine o'clock. I wasn't expecting anybody."

"I wasn't expecting me either, but I happened to drive by and saw you in your usual workaholic frenzy. In the window was a pair of long female legs poised on a ladder. I always brake for a good set of legs."

Alison gave him an unappreciative look.

He held up his palms in a defensive gesture. "I just came by to help. You look like you could use a hand."

Alison stared at him. She was torn between her need for help and her not wanting his help. It would be better for her if he would go flash his perfect smile somewhere else.

"Aren't you going to let me in?" he asked.

She shook her head. "I don't need any help."

"Maybe I should take a look for myself." Before she knew it, he was over the threshold. He surveyed the parlor and the dining room. He poked his finger into a section of exposed lath, noted missing screws on the window hardware, and wiggled a piece of loose molding. "This place has 'help needed' written all over it."

Alison grabbed a hammer and a finishing nail and marched over to the window with the offending molding. "Stand back," she warned. "You want to know how much I need help? Get ready for a demonstration."

She positioned the nail in the center of the wooden strip and poised the hammer over the nail head. Satisfied that she'd locked on to her target, she let the hammer fly. But what followed was not the musical clink of metal on metal, but the sickening smack of three pounds of steel on her thumb. Pain shot across her hand and up to her shoulder. The hammer clattered to the floor, barely missing her foot.

"Ow, ow, ow, ow!" She shook her throbbing thumb, then jammed it into her mouth.

"Let me see that," he said, tugging gently at her wrist.

She pulled it out slowly and examined it with growing dismay. The joint was swelling right before her eyes and her fingernail was taking on a dusky shade of blue. She wiggled it.

Stefan cradled her hand with his palm and inspected the thumb closely. "It's not broken. It probably just feels like it."

For an instant, she no longer felt the ache in the smashed digit. She only felt the warmth and strength of his fingers. She pulled her hand away and tried to recover some of her pride. "I really should get back to work."

He lifted a sleek brow. "I'd wrap a cool cloth around that thumb and call it a night if I were you."

"Well, you're not me."

His gaze swept to her toes and back to her face. "I'd go along with that. There's definitely a difference."

She folded her arms across her chest, ignoring the pain in her thumb. "Good night, Stefan," she said crisply. "Thank you for your offer of help."

His eyes shone with devilish determination. "I'm staying. Where's the screwdriver?"

She blinked. "I told you I didn't need any help."

"With that bum thumb, you need it more than when I got here," he countered. He glanced around the room and spotted a plastic tool caddie on the dining room table. He strolled over and contemplated its contents as if he were perusing a box of assorted chocolates.

Finally, he selected a Phillips screwdriver and tossed the tool up in the air with the confidence of a master carpenter. "Lift that bale. Tote that barge. Come on. Let's get to work."

Knowing she'd lost at her own game, she went to the parlor to finish washing the wallpaper sludge off the walls. He might have strong-armed his way into her house, but she didn't have to stay in the same room with him.

Her thumb throbbed. She sat down for a moment and stuck it in the bucket of water that she was using to wipe down the walls. It was then that she realized how achingly tired she was. By contrast, she could hear Stefan's footsteps in the next room. The man moved with an energetic and efficient cadence, which, in her weary state, she found perfectly annoying. Suddenly, the footsteps grew louder. She jerked her thumb out of the water and stood up.

"How's the thumb?" he asked, leaning against the door. A deepening shadow of beard defined his jawline. Alison was loath to admit that the stubble made him even more attractive in a rugged and masculine way.

"A little better," she said.

"Good. You might like to know that I've taken all the pulls off the windows, patched the hole in the plaster, and measured the cracked window for a replacement."

She stared at him, stunned at the speed at which he'd done it all. "Thank you," she said. "But you needn't feel obligated to stay."

He folded his arms across his chest. "Look, I didn't realize this place was in such bad shape. You need some help. Admit it."

"I'm getting some help. The electrician's coming next week."

"Electricians don't do windows or walls or floors for that matter. I do."

"Just what can you do?"

"I can drill, I can sand, I can miter, I can saw. I can carry a bucket, carry a ladder, and carry a tune. I can carry you."

She gave him a look of warning, then paused to collect her wits. "You give or throw away precious heirlooms. You toss out wonderful old letters. You abandon your aunt's baby grand as if it didn't have any more sentimental value than yesterday's newspaper. You live in a hotel without so much as a picture on the wall. How can you be Mr. Home Improvement when you have all the domestic inclinations of a hobo?"

He grinned, then his expression grew serious. "My father taught me a few things." An awkward pause followed. "Listen", he went on, "you've got a door that's sticking and a window that's jammed. I'll try to be quiet so I won't wake the little pirate."

"He's not here. He's spending the night with Mikey."

He lifted a brow in surprise, then looked at his watch. "It's past eleven. You weren't planning an all-nighter, were you?"

"I planned on getting some extra work done. I've

got a schedule to keep." She picked up her sponge and scraper and started on the wall again.

He seized her wrist. She turned to him in surprise. "What are you doing?"

His chin jutted out stubbornly. "I'm stopping you before you drop."

"I can't stop," she argued. His grip was firm but gentle.

"Yes, you can. Look at all the time I saved you. Go sit down. I'll bring you something to drink. What would you like?"

Alison took a deep breath and let it out slowly. How was it that this man was always working his way into her house and into her life? Was there a pest control company that specialized in dangerously attractive men? "Maybe I can take out a minute for some tea," she said grudgingly.

He released her wrist. "Now, you're talking."

"I'll put the water on." She plopped her sponge in the bucket.

"I'll put the water on," he insisted. "Just sit down."

In the parlor, Alison pulled the plastic drop cloth off the sofa and sank into one of the cushions. She almost groaned with relief. In the kitchen, Stefan bumped about clumsily. At least it sounded that way.

"Is everything okay?" she asked.

"Fine," he yelled. The sound of shattering glass followed.

Alison dodged a can of paint and sprinted into the kitchen. The remains of a teacup lay scattered around

Stefan's feet. He smiled sheepishly. "I failed to mention I'm not too good in the kitchen."

She grabbed a broom and a dustpan. "Some things just speak for themselves."

Stefan swept up the pieces while Alison finished making the tea. She put some vanilla wafers on a tray, along with cups and the ceramic teapot and carried it into the parlor. She set it on a cardboard box that she was temporarily using for a coffee table. She poured the tea and took in its soothing warmth. For the first time all evening, her muscles began to relax.

"Hearing any more bumps in the night?" he asked, appearing slightly amused. He sat at the opposite end of the old Chippendale, his long legs crossed at the ankles. His jeans fit snuggly over his thighs, revealing lean, muscular legs.

She shook her head. She wished he'd stop having fun with the subject. "Rosalie said Lura Bea still heard noises even after the mice were caught."

"She's right," he said matter-of-factly.

"And things were moved."

"That's what Aunt Lura Bea said," he acknowledged.

"Why didn't you tell me?" she asked, her concern growing.

"Because it didn't matter."

"Is there anything else you haven't told me?" she asked.

He set down his cup. "Relax and finish your cookie."

She sat up. "Stefan, I'd like to know."

"Here's what you should know." He laid his hand across the back of the sofa. His fingertips were tantalizingly close to the nape of her neck. "Lura Bea Yale was the most important person in my life after my parents died. She took in a seventeen-year-old boy who was utterly lost and alone. And during that year I lived with her, nothing strange happened in this house. The only strange sounds coming out of the house were the rock music I tormented her with. So there."

Alison smiled weakly. "I'm sorry. I know I'm being silly. It's just that I don't want Alex to be frightened of anything."

He touched a finger to the nape of her neck. Her blood surged alarmingly. "What you need is some rest."

She looked up at the ceiling, which begged for paint, and at the walls, which begged for paper. Suddenly, the room seemed as big as Texas. She struggled to reclaim her energy. "What I need is another cup of tea."

He looked at his watch. "It's one in the morning."

"It's time for me to get back to work."

He picked up her cup. As he started toward the kitchen Alison stretched out on the sofa and closed her eyes to steal some blissful seconds of rest.

When she opened them again, Stefan was tucking a blanket around her and a pillow under her head. Her heart lurched. She tried to sit up, but couldn't.

"Go to sleep," he said gently, kneeling beside her.

"I don't want to sleep," she argued. "I've got things to do and—"

Before she could finish, he took her head between his hands and touched his lips to hers.

Chapter Six

The kiss was firm, commanding, and quick, sending her senses into a spin. She stared at him speechlessly, unable to move. His gaze was smoky, his jaw firm. Before she could react, he kissed her again, this time softly, slowly, and with deliberation. He kissed her like a man for whom practice had turned kissing into an art.

Suddenly, he released her, leaving her dizzy and stunned and with her heart running a marathon in her chest. "Why did you do that?" she finally managed to say.

"I was kissing you good night." In contrast to hers, his voice was steady, his tone almost flippant. "To get you to stop before you drop, to make you quit arguing with me."

She took in a sharp breath and jumped to her feet. "Well, don't do it again."

A dark, well-shaped brow lifted slightly. He stood

up, folded his arms across his chest, and affected the classic wounded puppy-dog look. "You say that like you mean it." His words were tinged with irony, as if he didn't believe her.

Miffed, she parked her hands on her hips. "I do mean it," she repeated.

His mouth quirked with the barest suggestion of a smile. "Whatever."

Her blood fizzed. "I'm afraid you'd better go."

Her shrugged. "Good night." He turned, his footsteps echoing across the oak floor, and was gone.

Alison dropped to the sofa and took a deep breath to rein in her galloping pulse. She tried to take stock of what had just happened, but she couldn't fit the pieces together. All she knew was that she was mad— mad at herself, mad at him.

She was mad at herself for letting him kiss her. At the same time, she knew that something more powerful than she was had taken hold. It was an inner need that she thought had died along with Kevin. Tonight, he'd awakened it. And he'd made her feel vulnerable. She couldn't afford to care for another man who thrived on danger. Then he had the audacity to be so flippant about a kiss that had left her emotions in chaos.

The next morning, she awoke to the sound of the doorbell, followed by an impatient knock. She scrambled out of bed and down the stairs, pausing only long enough to throw on a terry cloth robe and to glance at the alarm clock she'd forgotten to set. It was eight o'clock. She'd overslept.

She threw open the door. Rosalie and the boys stood on the front porch. The boys wore stuffed, green toy boa constrictors wrapped around their necks.

"Eeek!" Alison clapped a hand over her mouth.

Alex and Mikey cackled, apparently satisfied with her reaction.

"They were selling them at the zoo," Rosalie explained. "They kept me up half the night playing with them. Remind me to have my head examined."

They stepped inside and Alison knelt to take Alex into her arms. He was holding a child's meal carton from a fast-food restaurant. "I missed you, sweetheart. Did you have a good time?"

"I had a whole bunch of fun."

"I'm so glad." Alison stood up. "Rosalie, I don't know how to thank you."

"No need to. I enjoyed the zoo as much as they did."

She invited Rosalie in for coffee. While the boys played with the train, Rosalie and Alison sipped their drinks at the kitchen table.

"Did you get a lot of work done?" Rosalie asked.

She nodded.

"I couldn't help but see a certain car in your driveway. Did you have a little help?"

Alison ran a hand over her disheveled tresses in an effort to tame them. "Unsolicited help," she said, feigning disinterest. She hoped that Stefan's sporty import was all that Rosalie saw.

"That was an interesting gesture on his part, considering that you don't seem to like him very much."

"Rosalie, he may be handy with a screwdriver, but he's also a collector of women. My mother warned me about men like him."

The older woman smiled and patted her on the arm. "Stefan is a good man. I've known his family for years; I've known him since he was a child. But I have to say that you're wise to be on guard. He may have a lot of women friends, but friends they'll stay. He made a choice a long time ago to build his life around his career. Once, there was a woman who thought she could change that. She was wrong."

Alison sobered.

"Well, I'd better be going," Rosalie said. "I brought Alex back with a full tank. He's already had his breakfast. Let me know if there's anything I can do from baby-sitting to running an errand."

"I don't know how I'm ever going to repay you as it is," Alison said.

"Don't talk that way. We're neighbors and neighbors help each other out."

After the boys said their good-byes, Alison took Alex into the kitchen for a cup of hot chocolate. "Tell me all about the zoo," she said exuberantly. Her son's shining eyes, rosy checks, and toothy little smile were like sunshine on her soul, making her all but forget Stefan Yale.

"Can I show you what I got, first?" he asked, reaching for the fast-food carton. The toy snake, which had a goofy, cross-eyed grin, was still coiled around his neck.

"Sure," she said, sitting beside him. "I'd love to see it."

He opened up the box and pulled out a shiny silver badge. "I'm a secret agent," he said, holding it out proudly.

Alison's heart constricted as she took it in her hand. It glittered under the lamp hanging over the table. "Where did you get it?"

"It came with my hamburger," he explained. "You could have a choice. Mikey got a truck. I wanted a badge."

"Was there a special reason you wanted a badge?"

He scrambled down from his chair. "Mom, would you help me put it on?"

"Alex, why did you want a badge?" she repeated.

"I want to be like Stefan. Stefan catches crooks."

Alison took in a deep breath. "That's dangerous, Alex."

"Yeah, but you can have fun too," he said, his face bright and innocent.

Alison wasn't eager to foster such a notion. He was only four. She didn't even want him to think about taking risks.

"Put it on, Mom," he urged.

She looked at the badge again, reminding herself that it was only a toy and that he was only a child. Little boys outgrew things and toys didn't last. Reluctantly, she began to pin it to the strap of his faded denim overalls.

"Mom, I wish Stefan could be my daddy."

Alison flinched, sending the pin through the overall strap and right into her finger. "Ouch!" she cried, jerking her hand away. A bead of blood slowly formed on the same digit she'd clobbered with a hammer.

Alex studied it with a mixture of horror and scientific interest. "You hurt yourself. How did you do that?"

She took a deep, shuddering breath. "I wasn't paying attention."

"Poor Mom," he said, patting her arm. The badge dangled from his chest. "Does your finger hurt real bad?"

"No," she said truthfully. The needle prick was nothing compared to the bomb of a question that Alex had just dropped on her. She chilled at the realization that it was too late to keep him from getting attached to Stefan. He'd already placed him on the highest pedestal of all. Unfortunately, the hero he worshiped couldn't have been more wrong for either of them.

Alison turned to the sink, stuck her finger under the tap, and blotted it dry with a paper towel. With an unsteady hand, she finished fastening the clasp. Alex gave the shiny badge with its "Secret Agent" inscription a look of satisfaction and squared his shoulders.

"Alex, about your wish," she began. "Not every wish can come true. Sometimes, it's best that they don't."

"What do you mean?" he asked, wide-eyed.

"Don't be wishing Stefan could be your daddy."

"Why not? He'd be a good one."

Alison shook her head. "We're doing fine by ourselves."

"Don't you like him?" he persisted. "He's big and strong and brave. Mikey said he can crush a soda can with one hand."

She clasped him by the upper arms. "Alex, don't talk about Stefan being your daddy anymore. He can be your friend, but that's all. His job is his family. That's the way it is."

The boy's chin dropped.

"Finish your cocoa and try not to think about it anymore," she said firmly.

Alison stuck his mug back in the microwave as he climbed back into his chair. With a pang of guilt, she set the reheated milk back in front of him. How could she expect Alex not to think about Stefan when she couldn't stop thinking about him herself?

During the next few days, Alison tackled yet another bedroom, one papered with cabbage roses faded almost to extinction. Their original pink hue was visible only behind the pictures hanging on the wall. She worked vigorously, trying to scrape clean from her memory Stefan Yale's kiss.

Rosalie and Mikey came in and out, and the parcel service came twice with items she'd ordered: a Victorian-style brass mailbox, brass heating-vent registers, and a kick plate for the front door. The meter reader stopped to chat, and the sudden appearance of warm, springlike weather brought by several strollers, including Betty and Heddy Marchand, eighty-year-old identical twins. Their house, a blue Victorian-style cottage with white gingerbread trim, was a block away. The spinsters brought with them a bouquet of jonquils from their garden and promised to come for tea once the inn was open. Notably absent from the mix of traffic was Stefan.

She found herself welcoming any distraction that kept her from seeing his face in her mind's eye. She didn't need him. Alex didn't need him, she told herself again and again.

Charlie, the electrician, was next to come. He turned out to be a she, a plump yet attractive blond whom Alison guessed to be in her mid-thirties. She introduced herself with a handshake. She walked with a jingle from the assortment of tools that she wore on her belt.

"So, you're the new owner of Lura Bea's house."

Alison nodded. "You knew her?"

"Everybody knew her. She never left the house without a hat and a pair of white gloves. Quite a lady. Quite a house. I haven't been in it in years," she said, eyeing the stripped and washed parlor walls.

"Were you one of her students?" Alison asked.

"I was until I took up volleyball. Poor Lura Bea. I never could get "The Blue Danube Waltz" right. As bad as I was, I was tempted to give it another try in high school. In fact, about that time, a number of girls took a sudden interest in taking piano lessons from Lura Bea."

"Why?"

"Her nephew. He'd come to live with her."

"Oh." Alison paused to absorb it. So the man's reputation as a lady-killer reached back practically to childhood.

"If she had been giving snake-handling lessons, I think girls would have signed up just to get into the house," she went on. "You've met him, I guess."

Alison nodded gravely. "Do you know him well?"

She shrugged. "He was in one of my classes in my last year of high school. Of course, like most girls, I would have liked to have know him better," she said with a laugh. "But he was a little hard to get to know. He'd just lost his mother. He'd lost his father a few years before that. It was hard on him. Then, years later, after he'd become an FBI agent, he lost his partner in an incident related to a case. That must be why he lives like there's no tomorrow, wining and dining an endless string of pretty girls and refusing to settle down." She pulled a pair of pliers out of her belt. "Well, I'd better get busy," she said cheerfully before trooping up the stairs.

Alison stood by the front door, forgetting about her own work. If Stefan didn't want to risk loss again and neither did she, why did she feel so unsettled? Was it because she liked the silken feel so his lips on hers? Was it because her son thought he could leap tall buildings in a single bound and bend steel with his bare hands? Was it because she knew that he'd disappear from her life as abruptly as he'd entered it?

For the entire day, Charlie crawled and thumped around in the attic, threading cables through the walls in the parlor and the dining room. She sawed rectangles for extra receptacles, and when she left, there was a film of dust and plaster powder over Alison's clean woodwork, the woodwork she'd scrubbed one night until she'd ached. She wasn't sure what the fuel had been behind her fury, but she suspected it had something to do with Stefan.

That evening, after making a quick supper of scrambled eggs and ham, she put Alex to bed and went downstairs to resume working in the parlor. This time, she'd hung sheets over the three windows that faced the street. That should tell Mr. Ladies' Man something.

She'd just snapped the first chalk line for hanging the first strip of wallpaper when she heard a car door slam. The sound of footsteps followed on the wooden planks of the wraparound porch. Her breathing stalled. She heard "Hi ho, hi ho, off to work we go" in Stefan's rich and familiar baritone, then the doorbell chimed brightly. He was obviously in a better mood than Alison, whose heart seemed to be running wildly in two directions at once. She turned on the porch light and threw open the door.

He came equipped with a caulking gun poised over his shoulder like a rifle. He wore the same jeans torn at the knee, running shoes that looked like they'd circled the globe during a monsoon, and a navy blue long-sleeved T-shirt with FBI printed on the front. His hair stuck up in places, his face was masked with stubble, and there were circles under his eyes. Still, he was undeniably handsome. He greeted her with a conciliatory smile. "You know, you shouldn't be just flinging your door open to strangers."

"You're not a stranger. You're just strange," she snipped. She was angry at him for popping back into her life; angry at herself for being almost, but not quite, glad to see him.

"You must have heard me singing. Does that mean you won't be requesting an encore?"

"Stefan, what are you doing here?"

"I'm going to caulk around the windows. If I don't, your heating bills will approximate those of Dante's Inferno." He stepped past her as if he had every right to be there and sized up the parlor as if it were a crime scene. "It's starting to come together. I hope you didn't mind my assistance the other night."

"The assistance, no." She looked at him coolly.

His gaze locked on hers. "I think I know what you're referring to."

"Now that you're here, I think we should have a talk," Alison said.

He crimped the corner of his mouth in a look that bordered on regretful. "Look, I've been doing some thinking."

He was interrupted by the sound of small footsteps descending the stairs. Alex appeared, wearing pajamas made to look like a baseball uniform. His sleepy eyes brightened.

"Stefan!" he cried, almost leaping into the man's arms. Alison's heart twisted in dismay.

Stefan plucked him up off the floor as if he were a toy. "Hey, pal, how's it going?"

"Fine. Where have you been, Stefan? I missed you."

Stefan set him back down. He turned toward Alison and lifted an eyebrow. "Did you hear that? *Somebody* missed me."

"Alex, what are you doing up?" Alison asked, pretending to ignore Stefan. "You should be in bed."

"I heard talking," he said.

"Sorry to wake you, old man." Stefan bent and gave the boy's shoulder a quick squeeze.

"It's okay. Where have you been?"

"I had to go out of town."

Alex's eyes shone with interest. "Did you catch some crooks?"

Stefan shook his head. "Not yet."

"I got a badge. Can I be your helper?"

Stefan ran a hand over his already rumpled hair and looked up at Alison for an explanation. The conversation between her fatherless son and a man who would rather face gunfire than be a father had already progressed further than she'd liked.

"His 'secret agent' badge came with a fast-food meal," she said.

"Let me show you," Alex said.

"Five minutes, Alex and it's back to bed," she warned.

He turned and ran up the stairs so excitedly that he stumbled slightly, sending Alison's heart scrambling to her throat. Undaunted, the boy paused only long enough to look over his shoulder. "Stay there. Promise you won't go away."

Stefan, who had poised himself for a dash up the

stairs, leaned against the newel post. "Promise. But only if you slow down."

He didn't. He sailed back down at a speed that sent his hair flying and thrust the shiny plastic oval about two inches from Stefan's nose. "See?"

Stefan examined it front and back and placed it on his own chest, pretending to admire it. Alex beamed. Alison stood back, barely taking a breath.

Stefan handed it back to him. "You take good care of that, Agent Perry."

Alex smiled shyly, a dimple appearing in one cheek. "Can I go with you sometime and help?"

Stefan's expression grew serious. A short silence followed. "I'm afraid not."

"How come? Would I get shot?"

Stefan glanced awkwardly at Alison. She wasn't sure she liked where this was going.

"Could you get shot?" Alex persisted.

"Alex, it's time to go back to bed," Alison interjected, taking his hand.

Stefan touched her shoulder. She felt her pulse jump. His gaze was dusky and entreating. "Let me explain."

Without waiting for a response, he crouched on one knee, and looked the boy in the eye. "I'm very careful. I've had very good training. Don't worry. The worst thing that ever happened to me was a cut finger."

Alison bit her lip, knowing there was so much more that he wasn't telling him, things that neither of them would want him to know. "Say good night to Stefan," she said, giving her son's hand a tug.

"But I want to play secret agent," he protested.

"It's too late to play."

"She's right," Stefan said. "Some other time. Good night, Alex."

"Night," he mumbled in disappointment.

Alison swiftly picked the boy up and carried him to his room. She held him tightly, as if she could protect him from even bigger disappointments that were sure to come.

After she put Alex to bed, she found Stefan seated on one of the bottom steps. He stood up and turned toward her, sticking his hands in his back pockets.

"Look, I hope you didn't mind. I didn't want him to go to bed thinking . . ."

Alison touched her fingers to her forehead. "He's only four. I don't want him thinking about such things."

"He needed to be reassured," he insisted.

She took a deep breath. "Thank you for trying, but down deep, I think both of us know that we can't offer him complete reassurance."

His mouth formed a grim line. "I'm sorry. I can't offer that to anybody."

"You know that in his eyes you're twelve feet tall. He wants to be like you," she said matter-of-factly.

He stared at her for a moment as if that were difficult to ponder.

She swallowed hard. "You're very good with him, but I don't want him to get too attached to you. I'm sure you feel the same way."

He nodded stiffly. "I'll be careful." An awkward pause followed.

"I really should get back to work," she said.

He crimped his distractingly sensuous mouth. "I was afraid you'd say that."

"What do you mean? You were the one who came armed with a caulking gun."

"I also came to make you take a break. You fell asleep on the job last time, remember? Put on the teapot. Coffee for me, thank you. Black and strong. I'll be back in a few minutes."

Before she could respond, he was out the front door. She took a deep breath and stared at where he'd been. She wished he'd never come and for an appalling instant, she caught herself wishing he'd never leave.

He returned ten minutes later, seemingly filling the parlor all by himself. He carried a red, white, and green carton. "Baklava from the Greek Kitchen," he announced. "They saved it for me. It's still warm. Tell me you can resist it."

His boyish enthusiasm made her smile. She thought of the terms of endearment he used for her son; she thought of the warmth of his lips on hers and her heart went soft.

In the kitchen, she unwrapped it. The scent of walnuts and honey almost made her swoon. "They must know you at the Greek Kitchen."

"I make a pass through occasionally," he said casually. "I used to go more often when their granddaughter Zena waited tables in her little jogging shorts."

Alison's heart braked. For just a little while, she'd allowed her head to turn to mush over a man who seemed to care about her well-being. Now, he'd given her an overdue reminder that he cared about the well-being of a good number of young, eligible women.

"Something wrong?" he asked innocently.

"Oh, no," she said lightly. She poured his coffee, accidentally overfilling the cup.

He quickly blotted it up with a paper towel. "What was that you were saying about our needing to have a talk?"

She slipped into the chair next to him. The rich dessert on her plate suddenly didn't seem so tempting after all.

"Stefan, you needn't feel obligated to help me. It's my house, my problem. You have your own responsibilities, your own life. I can manage on my own. I have up until now."

He put down his fork and leaned back in his chair. "This isn't about the kiss, is it?"

"There were two of them," she corrected.

His lower lip jutted out in the suggestion of a grin. "We can make it three if you like."

She placed her fork firmly on the table and got up. "The quantity isn't the issue. It's just that I don't take relationships as lightly as you do."

"I take them seriously, just not for long," he countered. "I don't need attachments, either, Alison. I'm always honest about that. As for the kiss, as for you and me . . . Call it admiration or whatever, but I just felt like doing it. Look, we're two adults who have something in common: You aren't ready for another man in your life, especially one with 'high risk' stamped on him like me. And I don't want a family for that very reason. So, don't you think that's a good basis for a perfect, no-nonsense friendship, no strings attached?"

Alison said nothing. She was thinking of his explanation for the kiss. Had it been nothing more than a misplaced smack on the cheek?

"A man and a woman can just be friends, can't they?" he persisted.

"What if there's a child involved?" she asked.

"So what if there is? Friendship can include children."

Alison took a deep breath. They weren't on the same wavelength after all. But to explain things to him would be to acknowledge her vulnerability.

"Enough of that, pal," he said, slipping his arm around her. "Finish your dessert."

Despite her insistence that Stefan not stay, he caulked the windows in four rooms while she hung wallpaper. They worked together in an uneasy rhythm. She was conscious of every step he took, every sound he made.

He sang softly, apparently showing her what a "pal" he could be. He sang bars from "Working on a Chain Gang," "Working in a Coal Mine" and "Working for the Man." Although the songs were intended for amusement, the richness of his voice caused unwanted stirrings within her.

"Finished," he announced finally. He juggled three

empty tubes of caulk, whirling and catching one behind his back.

She pretended to be unimpressed and was glad Alex wasn't there to see just the kind of trick that would further beguile a small boy. "Thank you, Stefan. Lucky for you, you don't need to come back. Everything is under control now. And thank you for the baklava. It was very nice of you. Sorry the girl in the jogging shorts wasn't there this time."

He shrugged. "Maybe some other time. Are you sure you don't want me to come back? The place is just screaming for an extra set of hands."

"I'm sure."

"Not even for a visit?"

"When the house is done."

He held out a hand as if they'd just sealed a business deal. "All right. If you need me before then, let me know."

Alison slipped her hand in his. The warmth of his touch sent her blood skipping with such a wild rhythm that she quickly pulled her fingers away. "Good night, Stefan."

"Good night," he said casually. "See you around."

Through the sheet covering the window, she could see his car lights disappear. She hadn't expected him to be so disaffected. Nor had she expected to feel so alone.

In the wee hours of the following morning, Alison lay in bed, too exhausted to get up and go back to work and too overwrought to sleep. She watched dots of light from the streetlight dance on the wall as they slipped through the tattered window shade. She listened to the now-familiar sounds of the old house—the hum of the refrigerator and the occasional rumblings from the heating register—and to the wild beat of her heart. In a few hours, Stefan would put on his gun to go out into an uncertain world. His decision to avoid emotional attachments would be reaffirmed. He was free to follow his heart and his heart led straight to his work.

In a few hours, she would pick up her tools and, in a symbolic way, continue to piece together a life that had been shattered when a military plane came spiraling out of the sky. Alison knew that no man lived without risks. Neither did she, for that matter. But Stefan took on more than the average person. She respected his feelings. She understood them, even. But she was drawn to him in a way that she couldn't seem to control, in the way that a moth is drawn to a flame. How wrong those feelings were. How right she was to try to keep him away.

Away, he couldn't inspire those worshipful looks in her son's eyes. He couldn't make her blood heat with his touch or give her kisses that meant nothing in particular. His absence, she vowed, would *not* make her heart grow fonder.

She closed her eyes and gave herself up to sleep. When she heard the noise, she thought it was a dream. Uneasily, she lifted her head from the pillow. It was the sound of footsteps, soft and halting.

"Alex?" she called.

There was no response.

She sat up and listened, her heartbeat quickening. She sensed that there was someone nearby, but nothing could be seen or heard. She got out of bed and went to Alex's room. She found him sleeping soundly, his teddy bear propped at the head of his bed like a sentry.

Cautiously, she checked the hallway and the room where he kept his toys. From the top of the stairs, she looked at the parlor and the dining room. Nothing was out of order but her thoughts. What had she heard? Was it the same thing Alex had heard during their first week in the house?

She crawled back into bed and listened, but the only sound was the beating of her own heart.

Chapter Seven

Alison strengthened her resolve to distance herself from Stefan. True to their agreement, he stayed away. And there were no more sounds except for one night when a shade scraped a windowsill. Alison had all but dismissed the idea that she'd heard footsteps at all.

In the meantime, small jobs turned into bigger ones. She accidentally broke a window when she tried to pry it open. Curtains she'd planned to salvage fell apart in the washing machine. The border that she'd bought for the dining room wallpaper seemed strangely to have disappeared.

She worked harder, faster. She worked to forget. She almost thought she could until one afternoon. She was sanding woodwork. Alex was playing with Mikey at Rosalie's. The radio was set on a classic rock station. At five o'clock, the music stopped for the news. Something was happening involving the FBI. Alison, feeling a slight chill, laid down her sanding block. An arrest had been made. The suspect, armed, had resisted. For moments after the report had ended, she sat very still.

For the next two days, she resisted the urge to call him. It was a foregone conclusion that he was safe. Besides, she thought wryly, there were probably so many women using that as an excuse to contact him that the circuits were likely jammed.

Just before she'd totally given up on the idea of calling him, her phone rang. "Alison Perry," she answered cautiously.

"Ms. Perry . . ." Despite herself, she was disappointed at the sound of a female voice. "It's Neva Creighton from the Convention and Visitors' Bureau. I understand you'll have your bed-and-breakfast open soon."

"May fifteenth," she confirmed.

"Oh, dear. I have three ladies who are desperate for a place to stay. They are members of the Cimarron class of 1949, which is having its 50th reunion May eighth through the tenth. It seems that the event is drawing a much bigger crowd than expected and because there's a convention in town that weekend—in addition to the class reunion—everything for miles is booked solid. Is there not just the tiniest chance that you could take them a few days before you're scheduled to open?"

Alison thought of the dreary, unfinished upstairs bedrooms, one with a carpet worn almost to the weft, and experienced a sinking feeling. "I'd love to, but . . ."

"They'll pay top rates," the woman interjected.

Alison's mind went to her anemic bank account, but still she thought the better of it. "I'm still renovating," she explained. "I'm afraid the accommodations won't be as nice as they would hope."

"I'll make that clear."

Alison hung up, took a deep breath, and ran upstairs. The rooms looked bleaker than she'd remembered. The wallpaper was stripped from one room, and the woodwork readied for painting, but the other lay yet in musty ruin. Before Alison could contemplate it any further, the phone rang again.

"Book them," the woman from the visitors' bureau said. "Don't worry if things aren't quite perfect. Your location is."

Alison, however, was not one to settle for "not quite perfect." She didn't want her first guests to give the Prairie Flower Inn bad or even indifferent reviews. It was a new business and its reputation was at stake. So, in less than three weeks, she had to do the near impossible—to get the house into shape. One thing was clear: She couldn't do it without help. She knew whose help she didn't need. She didn't need his woodsy scent and slanted smile. She didn't—couldn't—need him.

Rosalie came to her rescue. Alison convinced her, after much effort, that she must accept pay. They'd work while the boys played in an adjacent room.

Alison was astounded at how much could be accomplished with two extra hands. No novice to restoration, Rosalie hung up wallpaper like a pro. She scrubbed like a dynamo. She painted like a whirling dervish. Heartened, Alison dared to envision herself breaking through the ribbon of some domestic finish line, hanging white lace curtains and laying hooked rugs on newly refinished oak floors.

But a week into their team project, Rosalie called— from the hospital emergency room. Her car had been struck from behind. She returned home several hours later with her neck in a brace.

"I'm so sorry," she said. "The doctor said I should do the absolute minimum for the next week."

Alison gave the plump woman a hug. "Don't worry. The most important thing is that you weren't badly hurt."

"But you still need help," she said. "I know someone you can call."

She shook her head. "Do what the doctor said," she argued. "Thanks, but I think I can handle things by myself."

Rosalie looked at her as if she weren't quite convinced. She pulled an address book out of her purse and jotted down a number on the back of a gum wrapper. "This is a good friend of mine. Don't hesitate to ask."

By the end of the following day, Alison was exhausted, but no less determined that she could complete the job herself. The second upstairs bedroom lacked only a coat of soft blue paint before the floor refinishers came.

She sat at the dining room table, long after Alex

had gone to spend the night with Mikey, and went over a list she'd made. Thanks to Rosalie's help, she'd been able to check off half the items. Alison glanced up, then scribbled down another: *Get new wallpaper border.* The other wallpaper border had never turned up. Lura Bea had talked of things being moved but never disappearing.

She'd just gotten up to go to her sewing machine to start on a lace-trimmed bed skirt when the doorbell chimed.

She stopped in mid-stride. Just who would pop up at such an hour when she was struggling to squeeze a bit more productivity into the day? She knew the answer before she opened the door.

She smoothed down a tattered old white shirt of Kevin's she'd been wearing with a pair of equally old and frayed leggings and switched on the porch light. Her heart stumbled when she opened the door. He stood on the porch, his hands in the pockets of a weathered pair of chinos. His dark hair glistened with a light rain that had begun to fall. All she'd tried to do to convince herself that he wasn't such a heart-stopper, that his nose was a half size too large for his face, and that his hair sometimes looked like he'd just gotten out of bed, had gone for naught.

"Stefan, what are you doing here?" She tried to sound cross to mask her happiness that he was there at all, considering the treacherous paths he sometimes traveled.

"I heard about Rosalie. I thought I'd look around and see if there was anything I could do."

Alison took a deep breath and planted her hands on her hips. "But you promised . . ."

"And you said you didn't need any help," he reminded her pointedly. "After which you promptly turned around and hired Rosalie."

"I had to. I've got guests coming a week early."

"Now, I suppose you can kick back and drink mint juleps until they get here."

She placed her hands on her hips. "Stefan, go home, please. You have crimes to solve, women to chase."

Ignoring her plea, he grasped her by the upper arms, lifted her up, and set her aside so he could come in. "Let's not waste time taking potshots at each other. We've got work to do."

Alison stared at him, her tongue locked in her mouth.

Stefan surveyed the parlor, running a hand over the fresh wallpaper and inspecting the new electrical outlets. He moved fluidly, with the ease of a man in top form. He made the same inspection of the dining room.

"See? There's nothing that needs to be done."

Stefan touched the new brass heating registers on the dining room table. "I wouldn't say that."

Chagrined, Alison stared at him.

He picked up one of new window shades still in their packages. "Another little job yet undone."

"Stefan, really." She marched over to the buffet, picked up the gum wrapper that Rosalie had given her, and waved it at him. "This is the number of a friend of Rosalie's. This is a backup in case I need help. All I have to do is call. So, there."

He squinted at it, then grinned.

"What's so funny?"

"That's my number."

Her cheeks warmed. Her tongue locked. Why would Rosalie do this to her? She struggled for a response. "See, if I needed you, I would have called," she said finally.

His chin took on a stubborn set. "Alison, don't try so hard at not needing people. Everyone needs someone or something at some time in their life."

"That's interesting advice coming from someone who avoids permanent relationships like a four year old tries to avoid bath water."

"I have my work. That's something."

"I have Alex."

"And someday, Alex is going to grow up and leave home. There's got to be room in your heart for more than just him."

"No," she said, "not now."

He threw his arm around her shoulders and gave her a quick squeeze. Her pulse leaped.

"Maybe later," he said. "In the meantime, you've got me. I'll be your buddy if you'll let me. And if you're good, I'll fix an occasional leak or fling a bit of spackle now and then."

Inwardly, Alison flinched. A "buddy" like Stefan she didn't need. Few women probably survived a relationship with him their hearts intact. As for her, she was already on her way to being a casualty.

"What do you say we get to work?" he said with more cheer than she felt. "After a week like I've had, mashing my fingers with a hammer will feel good."

"What sort of week?"

"A bank robbery suspect gave us a hard chase."

"That was you?"

He responded with a look of surprise. "You know about it?"

"I caught something on the radio. I wondered if . . . The words seemed almost hard to say. "I wondered if you were okay," she finished.

He looked mildly pleased. "There you go. You're acting like a buddy instead of Ms. Iron Heart."

I was worried about everyone involved," she said stiffly.

"The suspect got bruised up a bit. I'll tell him you expressed your concern."

Inwardly conceding defeat, she snatched a screwdriver off the dining room table and thrust it in his hand. "If you'd like to get to work, you can start by taking off the old heating registers. The floor refinishers are coming Thursday, and when they finish, the new registers can be put on."

He glanced around the room. "Are you planning to move all this furniture out by yourself, Wonderwoman?"

"Rosalie and I . . . ." She stopped, suddenly reminded of Rosalie's incapacitation. "I mean—I can call a piano mover and the heavy stuff can be dragged by putting cardboard under it."

"Look, I know you consider me a womanizing, danger—loving nuisance and a pest besides, but I'll come over Wednesday night and help get this stuff out of the way."

She wanted to tell him no, but she was hardly in the position. "Thank you," she said instead. "That's very kind of you."

She worked upstairs while he worked downstairs, but he might has well have been in the same room. She was so distracted by his presence, the thumps and bumps of his movements below, that she accidentally rolled sky blue paint over the corner of a sparkling white window frame.

She let out a groan, then attacked it with a wet cloth, but before she could finish, she heard footsteps coming up the stairs. As she descended the ladder, Stefan appeared in the doorway. His hair was wet, and droplets of water ran down his face. In one hand was his shirt, soaked and wadded into a clump.

"What happened to you?" she gasped. She struggled to keep her gaze from wandering over his bare chest.

"I was attacked by an outdoor water hydrant."

Unsteadily, she got down from the ladder, almost missing the last step.

"I thought you might be able to spare me a towel," he said.

"Of course," she said, grabbing one from the adjoining bathroom. When she handed it to him, she blinked at the sight of his chest. It was broad, powerfully muscled, and covered with swirls of dark hair.

He ran the towel over his head, then his torso, and draped it around his neck.

She felt an urge to blot up a droplet at his throat that he had missed, but she stepped back. "I didn't know I had an attack faucet."

"It's cracked. It probably froze during the winter." His hair was spiked from the rough towel drying he'd given it, making him look boyish. "When I turned it on, water came out in all directions."

"What were you doing outside?"

"I needed to wash my hands and I didn't want to make a mess of your bathroom sink. I might add that I've got bad news about those heating ducts. They've got a few hundred cubic yards of dirt in them."

Alison frowned. "Great."

"That's an easy problem to solve. The duct people can have them cleaned out in no time."

She sighed. Her checklist seemed to be getting longer instead of shorter. "I'm sorry you got wet. Let me put your shirt in the dryer."

He lifted a muscled shoulder and let it fall. "Only if it's no trouble."

She took it from him and jogged downstairs to the utility room off the kitchen. Even wet, the shirt bore his scent of soap and freshly cut wood. She threw it quickly into the dryer and slammed the door shut.

When she got back upstairs, Stefan had finished cleaning the wet paint off the woodwork and had started recoating another wall. It was well past midnight.

"It's chilly. I think I might have something you can wear."

He turned and eyed the man's shirt that draped almost to her knees. "The shirt off your own back maybe?"

She folded her arms across her chest. "That's not exactly what I had in mind."

She went down the hall to her bedroom. She pulled another of Kevin's shirts out of her closet. A soft and faded purple twill, it had been his favorite. She handed it to Stefan.

He looked at it, his expression growing serious. "It was his, wasn't it?"

"It's all right," she said. "Put it on."

After a moment of hesitation, he slipped the towel from around his neck and handed it to Alison. He put on the shirt and buttoned it slowly. She was relieved when he closed up the narrow V exposing his chest.

"The one you're wearing was his too, wasn't it?"

She nodded. "I got in the habit of wearing his shirts when he was away on training exercises."

Stefan bit the inside of his cheek. "You still miss him, don't you?"

Alison nodded. "But two years have passed. It doesn't hurt quite as much."

"What was he like?"

"He was a good man, but a pilot first and a husband second. He lived to fly. Not even Alex's birth could change that."

"You came to accept it?"

"As best I could. With men like Kevin come certain conditions."

His gaze turned dark. "I understand."

"I thought you might."

He reached out and touched her elbow. "Understanding each other is part of what friendship is all about."

An awkward silence followed. Stefan began unbuttoning the shirt. "I didn't mean to make you uncomfortable."

She placed her hand over his. "No, leave it on until yours is dry."

He went downstairs and she stayed upstairs to finish painting the bedroom. Their footsteps and movements seemed to echo each others'. They were like two birds building a nest, she thought. Such irony.

Two nights later, he was back. With him were three teenagers, all members of the high school baseball team. With Alex safely out of the way at Rosalie's, the four of them moved the living room and the dining room furniture into the garage. They found the missing wallpaper border stuck behind the buffet. Alison, who had entertained the idea of Lura Bea's ghost having taken it, laughed inwardly at herself.

"Why wouldn't they let me pay them?" Alison asked, after the boys roared off in an old pickup truck.

"They owed me," Stefan explained. "I talked Aunt Lura Bea into donating some family property to the high school for a new baseball field. Try convincing a woman of a certain age that sports are worthy of philanthropy. She never understood the point of 'knocking a piece of leather around with a stick,' as she so quaintly put it."

"Neither do I," Alison said.

Stefan tossed a look at her that implied that she ought to know better. "Baseball is a metaphor for life. Sometimes there are hits, sometimes there are misses; sometimes we win, sometimes we lose, but the important thing is to keep on swinging."

He picked up an imaginary bat and lifted it into position. "You're in need of some serious fun. Throw me a pitch."

"What?"

"Come on. Give it a toss. You'd be surprised how good it feels." His voice echoed richly through the empty rooms. They seemed cavernous without Lura Bea's eclectic mix of furniture.

What she felt was ridiculous as she gripped her hand around an imaginary ball and hurled it toward him.

Stefan pretended to jump out of the way of a ball off course.

She parked her hands on her hips. "There. Are you satisfied?"

"One of the lessons that baseball teaches is patience."

"You're making me lose mine."

Amusement glittered in his eyes. "Try it again. Put some power behind it. Aim here," he said, gesturing to a spot above the floor.

Alison flung the ball toward it. Just as he swung his imaginary bat, the doorbell rang. Glad to end the charade, she made a dash for the door. It was Rosalie and Alex. A red stain ringed the boy's mouth.

"I saw the movers leave and figured it was safe to bring Alex home," she said.

As Alison thanked her, Alex darted past and rushed to Stefan. After Rosalie left, Alison turned toward them. She felt a twinge of concern as she noted the brightness in Alex's eyes.

"How's it going, partner?" Stefan asked.

"Look what I got," he said, pulling a sucker out of the bib pocket of his overalls. He pulled off the loose wrapper, showing the candy was already half consumed, then tried to hand it to him. "I saved some for you."

Stefan backed off slightly. "I appreciate that, buddy, but do you know what would make me really happy?"

The boy shook his head.

"To see you enjoy the whole thing by yourself."

A slow smile spread across the boy's face.

"Save the rest of it tomorrow," Alison suggested. "It's past your bedtime."

His face crinkled. "I want to show Stefan the tunnel I made for the train."

Make it fast," she said. "Stefan has to go to work tomorrow."

"Let's go," Stefan said, following the boy.

Alison sighed as they went upstairs. She remembered his promise to try not to let Alex become too attached. Then she realized that no matter how much he tried, he would likely fail. Perhaps he already had.

Alison paced nervously through the parlor, hearing their voices, but unable to understand what they were saying. Restlessly, she moved on to the kitchen where she busied herself by putting away the dishes and folding laundry.

Noticing that it had grown quiet, she started upstairs, only to meet Stefan coming down. "Where's Alex?" she asked.

"I put him to bed for you. He's waiting for you to come and kiss him good night."

Alison blinked in surprise. "How did you manage that?"

"I told him that secret agents needed to make sure they got plenty of sleep to keep their minds sharp and alert."

She gave him a grudging smile. "I'll be right back."

She found Alex sitting up in bed. His face had been wiped clean and he assured her he'd done a good job brushing his teeth. She rebuttoned his pajamas, which had been buttoned crookedly, kissed him on the forehead, and hoped he wouldn't have a certain dream that couldn't come true.

Stefan stood waiting for her in the parlor, his long legs spread slightly apart, his hands on his hips as he surveyed the room. He turned at the sound of her footsteps.

"We've turned a corner, don't you think?"

Alison, struck by the power of his presence in the empty room, struggled to respond. She wanted him gone so her heart would stop gyrating in her chest, so her blood would stop turning to fizz every time his gray gaze met hers. Yet she wanted him there. Finally, it was a sense of indebtedness that compelled her to decide. "To mark the occasion, I'll make some cappuccino."

"Good idea," he said, following her into the kitchen.

Out of habit, she reached for the radio as she started to work. Music from an oldies station softly filled the air. It was a sentimental song about a girl who had worn blue velvet.

Stefan leaned against an adjacent wall papered with faded green teapots and folded his arms across his chest. He studied her with interest as she poured coffee beans into the top of an electric grinder.

"Do you know what you are?" he asked.

She looked at him curiously. "A human being, if that's not too big of a stretch."

He smiled tersely. "You are the opposite of me."

"Thanks for the compliment," she said dryly.

He looked at her with a grudging smile. "You've got a kitchen with French roast coffee beans; I've got a backseat full of fast-food wrappers. Your idea of a good time is sitting home snuggled in front of a fire, into which you throw herbs and things to make it smell good; mine is out tracking suspects and getting dirty. You want to put down roots; I'm rootless. So, here we are, two improbable friends connected by an old house, one that's looking very good these days. I admire what you've done, Alison, and I admire you. You're a woman of resolve."

Alison set the grinder down on the counter. "Thank you, Stefan. Thank you for all the help you've given me."

He shrugged. "All you have to do is ask. And if there's anything Alex needs . . ."

"We have to be careful with that one," she reminded him.

He ran an index finger over the crease in his chin and nodded.

Suddenly, a cloud descended over her. Stefan, she realized, was saying good-bye in a backhanded way. The house was almost finished and there was nothing to hold him. She turned away and pressed the button on the grinder. The noise was a welcomed interruption.

"Alex is a great kid," Stefan said, once the grinding stopped. "He reminds me of the son of a partner I had not long after I got out of the academy. As it turned out, Lief died in the line of duty when his son was only five years old. It was not only hard losing a friend, but it took me back to losing my father in the same way. That was when I decided that a family of my own, and the trappings thereof, were the last things I needed. I don't want to cause anybody that kind of grief."

The room fell silent except for a ludicrously upbeat tune coming from the radio, something about an "itsy-bitsy, teeny-weenie yellow polka-dot bikini." Alison, unsettled, barely comprehended the words.

"Now, there's a song," Stefan said, his expression brightening.

Alison ignored him, putting the cappuccino machine through its paces. She set two cups topped with white froth on the table alongside a small plate of coconut macaroons—store-bought because she simply hadn't the time to make her own.

He sat across from her as if he belonged there. His large, square hands dwarfed the delicate rose-patterned cup as he took his first sip. "Great stuff. Your guest are going to drink it up."

She grinned despite herself.

"They're going to love your smile too. Stop being so stingy with it."

Alison rolled her eyes. "You've got a line for everything, don't you?"

He smiled back. It was a broad, white smile, almost shy, almost perfect except for its tilt. Then it faded. "I'm sorry if I said anything to make you sad. If it makes you feel any better, my partner's son ended up with a terrific stepfather."

"That's good to know," she said.

Soft, slow music welled up from the background. Alison brought up on her parents' music, recognized the song instantly as "A Whiter Shade of Pale." Stefan set down his empty cup, got up and reached for her hand. Her blood stirred.

"May I have this dance?"

Before she could reply, he pulled her up, turned up the volume on the radio, and led her into the empty parlor. He slipped his arm around her waist with the smoothness and confidence of a man who not only knew his way around a dance floor, but who knew his way around women. When he pulled her against him, she was afraid she would melt.

He took her slowly over the bare, oak floor, her

hand cradled in his. His cheeks was rough and heated against her temple. Her fingers ventured to the nape of his neck. "Buddies," it seemed, wouldn't be dancing like this.

They danced in silence, her heart beating so loudly that she was afraid he could feel it against his chest. The magnetism of the moment was so strong that they danced even though the music had stopped. Stefan's hands slipped to her shoulders. She knew what was going to happen next, but she lacked the will to stop him.

He touched his lips to hers. The kiss was hardly more than a whisper, a tease, a nibble, but it left her heart pounding wildly in her chest. It left her aching for more.

He stepped back slightly, his hands dropping from her shoulders. His eyes were murky, the color of the ocean on a cloudy day. "Go to bed, queen of drudge. Promise me you won't drag out the rollers and trays again after I leave."

Alison responded with a dazed nod.

"That's my girl." He bent down and grazed her cheekbone with another kiss. "Sweet dreams." Then he was gone.

The heat of the kiss lingered long afterward. But what was just a simple kiss to him had just turned her heart inside out.

Chapter Eight

During the next week, the old house underwent a final and sparkling transformation. The oak floors were refinished to a honey hue. Lura Bea's old Turkish rugs were cleaned and put down. The furniture and the piano were moved back in and polished, and crisp, white lace curtains were hung. Alison added her own needlepoint pillows, brass candlestick collection, vintage books, and blue and white porcelain.

She surveyed the parlor and dining room with satisfaction and no small amount of relief. She took pleasure in the finished details. It looked like home. Yet in every room was a reminder of Stefan, from the sound of the doorbell to the windows he'd repaired.

Once the house was finished, he'd seemingly vanished. Reason told her that it was best that they stay apart. Yet her defiant and irrational heart yearned for him.

Alison busied herself getting ready for her first

guests. She planned menus, ordered flowers, bought handmade soaps, and gave Alex a refresher course in manners. As busy as she was, Stefan still crept into her thoughts.

On the day her guests were to arrive, the doorbell chimed. Alison opened the door to find a floral delivery woman with a dozen red roses.

"There must be some mistake," Alison said. "I ordered mixed flowers." She'd selected varieties that were as close as she could get to prairie flowers.

"No, ma'am," she insisted, "the card says they're for you."

Curiously, she took them inside and placed them on the piano. She tore open the tiny envelope that came with them. *The best to you and the Prairie Flower Inn. I'll drop by this evening.* Stefan's name was signed in a broad, masculine scrawl.

Her heart thumped. She repositioned the vase, putting it on a fringed, white scarf on which she'd also placed family pictures in assorted frames. The roses were perfect, making part of her wish that he were there. Another part of her wished he'd be transferred to Alaska, where there would be a shortage of women to chase.

Her guests arrived at just after four in a cloud of perfume and chatter. There were three: Lillian Hargrove, treasurer of the Class of '49; Pansy Bartholomew, voted "most likely to succeed," and Nelda Lou Reinhardt, band-queen attendant.

Lillian was a tall, thin, nervous woman with a stiff,

silver bouffant. Petite, red haired Pansy moved with the brisk, efficient air of the retired accountant that she was, and Nelda Lou was a buxom, blond great-grandmother with brightly rouged cheeks.

"What a lovely place," Nelda Lou marveled, sizing up the parlor. "I'm so glad you were able to take us."

"I'm very pleased to have you," Alison said. She was dressed in a black-and-white checked linen jumper and black ballet flats. Against his will, Alex wore dark blue pants and matching suspenders, a white shirt and a navy, red, and yellow bow tie with a puppy-and-kitten print. He tugged uncomfortably at his collar.

"What a darling child," Pansy cooed.

Alison introduced him to the three women.

Suddenly, purses popped open and pictures of grandchildren flew out, followed by a flurry of exchanges. "Can you believe we're grandmothers?" Nelda Lou asked. "It seems like only yesterday that we were walking home from school together and talking about boys."

"You're still talking about them," Pansy quipped, setting off a twitter of laughter. "Except they're not boys anymore."

Nelda Lou's red-glossed mouth twisted into a wry smile. "A widow's entitled to have her fun, isn't she? And if you want to know, my horoscope says that I'm on the brink of a major love affair. Who knows who might show up—single again—at this reunion?"

Pansy touched Alison's elbow. "Forgive us. We're just silly girls."

Alison smiled. "Be silly all you like."

Lillian, quieter than her giddy companions, stepped over in her sensible suede oxfords and placed a hand on the piano. "This was Lura Bea's, wasn't it?"

Alison nodded. "When I bought the house, I also bought the contents."

"My lands," she marveled, running her hand over the polished black surface. "I took lessons on this piano. I started at six. I was one of her first pupils."

"You're welcome to play it again, if you like," Alison said.

"I'd love to after I freshen up a bit."

"Girls, let's bring in our luggage and get ready to do the town," Nelda Lou enthused.

They scrambled out the door to a red sports car parked at the curb. Nelda Lou opened the trunk and the door on the passenger's side and pulled out more suitcases than Alison would have guessed the car could hold. It took two trips to haul it all in.

She showed them to their rooms, which were bright, airy and smelling of wax and potpourri. Tiny boxes of chocolate, tied with gold ribbon, rested on lace pillow shams. In every room were miniature welcome baskets of dried fruit. Much to Alison's relief and pride, the women were delighted.

Twenty minutes later, they were back in the parlor for coffee and cinnamon scones. "Breakfast is served from seven to ten in the morning," Alison explained, handing them printed menu cards.

Lillian, who nibbled nervously at her scone, squinted at her card. "Oh, dear. I forgot to mention that I have certain dietary requirements. I can't eat anything with eggs in it and I'm allergic to orange juice. And whole wheat plays havoc with my system."

Alison experienced a withering sensation. "How about yogurt and fresh fruit?" she asked pleasantly.

She winced. "Lactose intolerant."

"What would you like, then?"

"Just plain toast and jelly, as long as it's not orange marmalade, of course, and it doesn't have butter on it. I'm sorry to be such a problem."

"I'll be happy to accommodate you in any way I can," Alison said.

Leaving them gossiping under the brass dinning room chandelier, Alison retreated to the kitchen to check on Alex. He'd shed his bow tie—it was looped over the back of his chair—and he was finishing up a page in his coloring book.

"Mom, do I have to dress up tomorrow too?"

"No, Alex." Before she could explain further, the doorbell chimed.

She hurried past the dinning room to the entryway and found Stefan standing on the front porch. Although he'd told her that he'd come by, her heart kicked at the sight of him. He was suited handsomely in dark gray. His white shirt was unbuttoned at the throat and his purple print tie had been yanked loose. His wind-tousled hair gave him a careless air.

"Hello, Stefan . . ."

The corner of his mouth lifted in a slight smile. "I came by to congratulate you and to see if there's anything I can do to make opening day a little easier."

The clatter of small footsteps sounded behind her.

"Like baby-sit for instance."

"Oh, boy! Stefan!" Alex cried.

"Hey, sport," he said, ruffling the boy's bangs. "What's up?"

"We've got three grandmas staying at our house."

Alison cut in before he had a chance to describe them. His descriptions tended to be embarrassingly honest. "One of them took piano lessons from Lura Bea," she interjected quickly. "Let me introduce you."

When Alison walked through the open French doors leading to the dinning room, all eyes went not to her, but to the man following her. Nelda Lou's gaze turned to glitter.

As Alison paced through the formalities, even Lillian's nervous, strained look was replaced by a look of mild pleasure.

Nelda Lou patted her blond bouffant with her palm. "You're Lura Bea's grandnephew? Oh, my. Would you look at that!"

A tight, self-conscious smile touched Stephan's lips and a perverse twist of amusement spiraled through Alison as she watched him squirm under the spotlight of their inspection.

"Honey, I remember when you were just a little ol' bitty thing still in diapers," Pansy said.

Alison thought she actually saw a tinge of color on his cheekbones.

"It was a pleasure to meet you ladies," he said, backing off.

"The pleasure was all ours," Nelda Lou said.

In the safety of the kitchen, Stefan loosened his tie even more and looked at Alison. "They're certainly friendly enough."

She gave him a tight-lipped smile, but said nothing.

He pulled out a chair and took a seat next to Alex. He placed a hand on the boy's shoulder. "Boldness has its place, but we men usually like a little mystery in a woman. We like to have to to guess what she's really thinking, right my lad?"

"Yep," Alex agreed with gusto.

Alison wrinkled her nose. "Are you trying to corrupt my son?"

"It was just a little man-to-man."

Alison cast him a chiding look.

"Other than my annoying you, how's your day going?" he asked. His gaze was probing, teasing.

She sighed. "You're not really annoying me. The roses are beautiful. They were a wonderful surprise. Thank you."

"Don't forget my offer to baby-sit."

"Can, he, Mom, please?" Alex interjected. He turned to Stefan. "We can color together and you can tell me about bad guys. You can color, can't you? If you can't, I'll teach you. You gotta stay inside the lines."

Stefan smiled lopsidedly at the boy, then turned and looked at Alison inquiringly.

"It's very thoughtful of you to offer," she responded, "but so far, I'm managing just fine. You've done so much as it is."

He shrugged. "Just thought I'd ask," he said, getting up.

She realized with alarm that she didn't want him to go. "How was your day, Stefan?" she asked softly.

"Mired in paperwork. I never left the office."

He was safe, a voice inside her shouted with gladness.

"What's up for tomorrow?"

"Who knows?" he asked. "That's what makes it exciting."

And dangerous, she thought darkly.

He slipped an arm casually around her shoulder and pushed open the swinging door separating the kitchen from the dining room. The grandmas were gone.

He dropped his arm as nonchalantly as he'd placed it there and surveyed the empty room. "Looks like the coast is clear."

Alison, however, was thinking not of the women, but of the way his touch had left her skin tingling, as they crossed into the parlor.

"It looks terrific, Alison, like a real home. All you need now is a husband to sit by the fireplace and a baby to toddle over the rugs."

His words, too close to the truth, smarted. She shook her head in denial. "I was rather thinking about a nice, friendly dog."

"Don't rule out a nice, friendly man."

"Stefan . . ." she cautioned with a tone of warning.

His gray eyes danced with amusement. "As a friend, I'll keep an eye out. I hear we've got a new agent transferring in."

"No," she said firmly. "No matchmaking. Especially with daredevils."

The light in his eyes died. "I'm sorry." He touched her arm. "Forgive me."

"It's all right," she said, gently moving his hand away.

"I'd better go," he said softly. He stepped back into the kitchen to say good night to Alex, then, with a wave, walked out the door.

She watched him leave, her heart raw. He was kind, generous, and considerate, and just the right fit for the overstuffed chair in the parlor. But the unspoken words between them were that he was not the right man to fill it.

Alison was adding the last ingredient—a teaspoon of vanilla—to the waffle batter when she heard her guests come down the stairs. It was just before nine and they were right on schedule. She smoothed down her white chef's apron and greeted them in the dining room.

"Good morning. I hope you rested well."

Nelda Lou, who had already made lavish use of her makeup kit, responded with a coral smile. "I did, but of course, I'm used to staying out late."

"My bed was just right," Pansy said, "but, you know, I woke up hearing strange noises."

Alison's breath caught.

"You heard it too?" Lillian asked. Her face was pinched and there were deep circles under her eyes.

"What sort of noises?" Alison asked.

"Like footsteps, someone walking around my bed," Lillian said breathlessly.

Pansy nodded. "Yes, that was it, except the noise seemed to be coming from the stairs."

"If it was a man, I'm sorry I slept through it," Nelda Lou said with a cackle.

Lillian was unmoved by the joke. "I woke up feeling as if someone had been standing over me. It was strange."

Pansy turned to Alison. "What do you suppose it was?"

"It could have been the normal squeaks and groans of an old house. Or . . ." She took a deep breath to infuse lightness into her voice. "It could have been a ghost."

A deep laugh rolled from Pansy's ample belly, forcing the others to smile. Alison felt like hugging her.

"Vanilla waffles are coming up," she said, happy to change the subject. "They're served with maple cream and fresh strawberries, and made from my grandmother's recipe. Lillian, I have toast and a special raspberry jam for you."

Lillian nodded stiffly.

Alison escaped to the kitchen, where Alex was watching cartoons on a small television set. Her heart raced as she poured the juice, orange for Pansy and Nelda, and prune for Lillian. She was so unsettled by what the women had told her that she accidentally overfilled Lillian's glass. She could no longer pass the phenomenon off as a dream, a little boy's natural fear of the dark, or Lura Bea's overactive imagination. Lillian and Nelda had experienced it too.

Yet it all seemed to be forgotten as the women ate their breakfast, two of them with gusto. Alison overheard them chattering eagerly about the events of the day—a "get-reacquainted coffee," a picnic lunch on the school grounds, a dance in the gym, and a band playing "all the old songs."

Late in the afternoon, they came back to the inn to rest up for the night's festivities. But rather than appearing tired, they looked charged. Lillian, if anything, looked a little wild-eyed.

"Alison, you weren't joking about a ghost, were you?" Pansy asked.

She blinked. "What do you mean?"

"An old friend at the reunion said Lura Bea claimed for years that there was a ghost in this house, but nobody would believe her. She said that things even moved—mysteriously."

Lillian nodded. "Footsteps, that's what she heard, just like we did."

Even Nelda Lou, who had been a skeptic just that morning, looked concerned. "Who knows? Nobody has proven there *are* ghosts yet it hasn't been proved that there aren't. If enough people believe something, maybe there's some truth to it."

"I know about the stories," Alison acknowledged, "but as far as we can determine, they're just that— stories. I think people are unwilling to let go of them because they make life more interesting in a sleepy town." She was pleased with her logic. She even made herself feel a little better.

Nelda Lou nodded, but Lillian and Pansy looked scarcely appeased.

"There were some toys of my son's that were scattered and we discovered that there were mice in the attic," Alison added.

"Mice?" Lillian gasped, clamping a hand over her mouth.

"Don't worry. They've been caught."

Lillian's pinched expression relaxed somewhat.

Alison served them cappuccino before they went upstairs to rest before an evening of dinner and dancing. Lillian sat at the piano and knocked out a shaky rendition of "Don't Sit Under the Apple Tree with Anyone Else but Me." It was followed by "Für Elise," which she said had been Lura Bea's favorite, and required of all her students.

Alex, still wearing the secret agent badge that Alison had hoped he'd tire of, abandoned his story books on the parlor floor and stood by the piano to listen. When Lillian finished with an uncharacteristic flourish, her friends applauded and the tension in the room lifted.

That night, Alison lay in bed and strained at every sound. The only footsteps she heard were those of the three women ascending the stairs shortly after midnight. The only sound of any significance was a hiccup followed by a muffled giggle.

Shortly after three, she was started awake by a light

rapping on her door. She stumbled out of bed, threw on a robe and opened the door.

"I heard it again." Lillian whispered, her voice cracking with anxiety.

Alison's heart took on a brisk cadence. "What did you hear?"

"Footsteps," she choked. "Just like before. It was like somebody was there."

Alison touched her hand to her throat. "Let's go take a look."

As she feared it would be, the exercise was futile. The window was closed, eliminating the possibility of a breeze causing the noise. She tugged on the bed frame and sat on the mattress, but what little sound there was didn't give the effect of footsteps.

"I'd know if the noise was coming from the bed," Lillian said. "It was footsteps, I tell you, as sure as I'm standing here."

Alison swallowed hard. "I know there's a logical explanation for this," she said, trying to convince herself as well as Lillian. "Please try to get some rest. Leave your door open if you like. I'll even leave the hall light on."

She twisted her hands nervously, then sat on the edge of the bed. "All right. Sorry to be a bother."

"My guests are never a bother," she said reassuringly. "Lie down, take ten deep breaths and let them out very slowly. It will help you get back to sleep."

Alison tried to follow her own advice, but sleep never came. She'd always dismissed the notion of ghosts, but now she couldn't. As long as her guests weren't comfortable, she couldn't be either.

That morning, Lillian was absent from the breakfast table.

"Is Lillian all right this morning?" Alison inquired.

Nelda Lou and Pansy exchanged awkward looks. "She's a little out of sorts," Nelda said.

Suddenly, footsteps sounded behind her. Alison turned to find Lillian looking pale, tired, and pinched. Alison felt a twist of mild alarm.

"I'm sorry, Alison," she said, "but I can't stay here another night. Those noises are just playing havoc with my nerves. I think Lura Bea knew what she was talking about when she said there was a ghost in this house."

Alison's heart banged against her ribs. "Isn't there something I can do to put you at ease?"

"I wish there was," she said, twisting one of the buttons on her tailored white blouse. "But the girls and I were talking and decided it might be more restful to spend our last night down at the hotel. Some friends have offered to let us stay in their rooms on cots."

The other two cast apologetic looks toward Alison. "It's not that we're unhappy with the Prairie Flower. It's lovely and the food is delicious," Nelda Lou quickly added. "And you're just the sweetest hostess. But we've been friends for more than fifty years and we're sticking together still. If Lillian wants to go to the hotel, that's what we'll do."

Disappointment settled leadenly in Alison's gut. "I'm so sorry to see you go, but I understand."

By noon, their suitcases had been crammed back into Nelda's little red sports car and they were gone. Alison had grown accustomed to Nelda's throaty laughter reverberating off the walls. Now the only sounds remaining were the clicks and clacks of Alex's train as it revolved around the tracks on the kitchen table.

Two days later, an acquaintance of the three women called to cancel her reservation for later in the spring. No reason was given. Considering the fresh spate of stories about the Prairie Flower's "ghost," there was little need to wonder.

Alison worried about the long-range impact such stories could have. Even more troubling was that she couldn't dismiss them. She and Alex had heard the same noises.

She couldn't blame Stefan for ruling out Lura Bea's claims and even her own. He was an investigator who relied on solid evidence. Yet who else could she go to? She didn't want to bring him and his gorgeously lopsided smile back into her life, but she didn't know what else to do.

Stefan agreed to come on Friday night. He brought a pepperoni pizza—Alex's favorite. He wore a pair of faded jeans, torn at one knee, a pair of running shoes, and a navy blue T-shirt with a logo on the front and *FBI* across the back.

He greeted Alex by balancing the pizza box on his head and slowly turning a circle. He acknowledged Alison with a dancing gleam in his eyes. Out of Alex's earshot, he asked: "Had any more guests—the kind you can pass a hand through?"

"Be amused all you like," she said.

He smiled that smile and despite everything, it still turned her heart to liquid. It began at one corner of his devastating mouth and tweaked slightly upward. "Thank you. I will. But for right now, let's have some pizza."

Alison struggled to finish one piece while Stefan and Alex ate heartily. They were two peas in a pod, she thought sadly, a boy who wanted to play and a man with a playful spirit.

By the time the pizza had been reduced to a few remaining crumbs, it was Alex's bedtime. When the boy resisted, Stefan bribed him into bed by teaching him a karate maneuver and promising him more lessons.

Alison turned out the light in the boy's room and went downstairs. Stefan, who had stepped out to his car, returned, carrying a duffel bag.

"Are you going to tuck me in too?" He dropped the bag by the door.

Alison, straightening her spine, pretended she didn't hear him. "I know you're very skeptical about this, so I appreciate your willingness to come and do some more looking around."

"I can't promise any answers, Alison. I went through this with Lura Bea."

"I understand."

He picked up the bag again and slung it over his shoulder. "I'll put this is your room."

She blinked. "My room?"

He nodded. "I'm spending the night in your room—with you."

Her heart scurried to her throat. "You are not."

An aggravating twinkle flashed in his eyes. "How else do you expect me to check out the ghost?"

Alison's mouth opened, but the only sound that come out was a squeak. "Stay in the room where Lillian slept," she finally managed to say. "The noises were in there too."

"How will I know when I hear them?" he volleyed back. "I'm a sound sleeper. I'm going to need some help on this."

"You'll know. You'll wake up feeling as if someone has been standing over the bed."

He raised an eyebrow. "I wouldn't count on it."

She took in a sharp breath.

"Trust me. This is the best way to go about this. You sleep on the bed and I'll sleep on the floor."

Alison chewed the inside of her cheek, staring at him. This was more complicated than she'd expected. "Try not to disturb Alex. I don't want him to think . . ."

"Think what?" he asked playfully.

She leveled a reproachful gaze at him. "Come on. Let's go up and get you settled down."

Alison turned out the downstairs lights except for one in the entryway and secured the front door. Stefan followed her upstairs, his duffel bag resting on his shoulder. Despite their attempts to be as quiet as possible, the old stairs creaked and groaned.

Her room was at the end of the hall next to the stairs that led to the attic. She flipped a switch and light flooded softly over faded, rose-patterned wallpaper and yellowed lace curtains.

Stefan entered, his presence an unspoken intimacy. He was in her bedroom, a private space she'd grown unaccustomed to sharing. He stood on a small hand-hooked rug at the foot of the bed and set the duffel on the floor.

"This was Lura Bea's room. It looks exactly as she left it."

"I'll redo it when I can," Alison said stiffly.

Stefan, taking on a professional demeanor, paced around the room, examining the walls and the ceiling. Softly, he paced back and forth at the foot of the bed. "Is this what it sounded like?"

She nodded. "But the steps were lighter and seemed to come from the ceiling and the floor."

He looked at her warily. "Are you sure you don't still have mice?"

"Stefan, mice don't sound like this. Mice don't make you feel as if someone were standing over you."

He bit his bottom lip, but said nothing.

"You're thinking I'm nuts, aren't you?"

A hint of a smile appeared on his lips. "I'm trying to keep an open mind."

Alison turned and went to the linen closet where she fumbled for sheets and blankets. Her blood warmed alarmingly when she thought of all that masculinity on the loose in her bedroom.

With the no-nonsense efficiency of a hotel maid, she

unfolded one of the blankets into a pallet and laid it against the wall, as far away from the bed as possible.

"Hey, I'm not contagious," Stefan said, nudging the blanket closer to her bed. He grabbed the rest of the bedding and finished the job.

She punctuated his performance by tossing him a lace-trimmed pillow from her bed. "Sweet dreams," she said.

"Not so fast. This is one night I'd like to savor."

"In case you don't know it, that line sounds a little ragged around the edges."

His mouth twisted slightly. "Why don't you go take a nice, relaxing soak while I keep watch for our friend from the netherworld?"

Alison did an about face and went to her chest of drawers. Before pulling open her underwear drawer, she looked over her shoulder. He was watching with interest. "Would you kindly turn your head?"

He complied just long enough for her to pull from the bottom of the drawer an old pair of pajamas that she'd had since college. Styled like a man's, they were striped and boxy and had faded to an especially unattractive shade of greenish yellow.

"Save some hot water for me," he said as she left the room.

Ignoring his request, Alison opened the hot water tap a few minutes later to full throttle. A cold shower might do the man good.

She stayed in the tub a good fifteen minutes in an attempt to bridle her senses. When she got out, she was pink from head to toe and her heart was still at a gallop. With her pajamas buttoned to the collar, she padded self-consciously back to her room.

Stefan, sitting in an old wicker rocker, rose to his feet. "Charming."

"Isn't it time for your cold shower?" she quipped.

His eyes twinkling, he picked up his duffel bag. The instant he left the room, she quickly threw back the covers on the bed and crawled in. Leaning on a pillow propped against the headboard, she rifled through a decorating magazine, but she couldn't concentrate even well enough to study the pictures. In the adjoining bathroom, the water in the shower hummed and sluiced. She thought of him wet and glistening, then tossed down the magazine in futility.

A few minutes later, Stefan strode through the bedroom door as boldly as Alison had entered shyly. He wore only the bottom half of a pair of pale blue cotton pajamas, their drawstring tied loosely around his well-toned midsection. His shoulders were square and his muscles well-defined. The hair on his chest glistened. Just above the deepening shadow of his beard was a rosy glow that extended to his cheekbones.

Suddenly, Alison realized that she was staring like a schoolgirl. Worse, he'd caught her at it.

"Surprised I don't have a tattoo—a snarling wolf or a fire-spewing dragon?"

She felt her color deepen. "Maybe," she said stiffly.

He placed his hands on the bed's curved foot piece. His chest was as unavoidable as a movie screen from a front-row seat. "Couldn't do anything that radical. If

I did, Lura Bea would come back from the grave and swat me with one of her white gloves."

"I thought you didn't believe in ghosts."

"We'll know more about that after tonight."

He came around and sat on the opposite side of the bed, sending her heart leaping in alarm.

"What are you doing?"

"Checking to see if the bed makes noises—as in stepping noises." He sat down on the opposite side of the bed and shifted his weight, but the mattress emitted only the normal squeaks.

Alison threw back the quilt and jettisoned away from him. But before she could get out of bed, her left foot caught in the sheet. She struggled to maintain her balance, but gravity won out and she landed soundly on her back side. He jumped to her aid.

"Are you okay?" His eyes went dark with concern.

"I will be if you keep off my bed, at least while I'm in it."

He pulled her up off the floor, his hands lingering at her waist. "I'm sorry. I was just doing my job."

Alison backed away from his grasp. Brushing off the seat of her pajamas, she gave him a skeptical look.

"I promise to be a good boy for the rest of the night. I'll go to bed right now." Dutifully, he lay down on the pallet and pulled the blanket up over his head. All that was visible were his feet.

"Good night, Stefan."

He exposed his face. There was a hint of a smile on his lips. "Good night."

Alison got into bed and turned out the light. Although Stefan was a good eight feet away, she was very aware of his presence. Her heart beat too fast for her to sleep. She lay as still as possible. As her eyes adjusted to the darkness, she could see Stefan's long form under the window, his body illuminated slightly by tiny bands of light filtering through the blinds. She could hear him tossing.

"Stefan, are you awake?"

"You didn't hear anything, did you?"

There was something comforting about hearing his voice in the darkness. "No. When did Lura Bea first come up with the idea that the house had a 'presence?' "

"If she did, she didn't tell me until years later. She may have earlier been trying to protect me, although I was quite capable of protecting both of us."

"You never heard anything—ever?"

"No, never."

Alison sank against her pillow and studied the motes of amber light dancing on the ceiling until they grayed into oblivion.

When she awoke at dawn, Stefan was gone. The blankets on which he slept were neatly folded. On the dresser, was a note:

I wanted to make sure I left before Alex got up. I don't recall having fallen asleep at all last night, so I'm reasonably confident there were no unusual noises.

Alison felt a twinge of frustration. Somehow, she had to make him believe her. Her eyes went to a small arrow at the bottom of the note. She turned it over. *P.S. Did you know you talk in your sleep?*

She pressed her fingertips to her forehead. No, she didn't know, she thought with dread.

Alison spent the day doing basic planning and bookkeeping, but she found it difficult to concentrate. She had two guests coming soon, a retired professor who collected books on the Old West, and elderly sisters who studied Victorian architecture as a hobby. She hoped they didn't go fleeing for the exits as well. Rosalie had reported much to Alison's chagrin, that just the other day, the senior citizens' center had been abuzz with conversation about the return of Lura Bea's "ghost."

Late that afternoon, while Alex was at Rosalie's watching a Disney video with Mikey, the doorbell rang ceremoniously. Alison switched off her calculator and got up from the dining room table to answer the door.

It was Stefan. The sleeves of his light blue shirt were rolled up and his burgundy tie was loose. His service revolver was secured at his waist. "I have an idea I wanted to talk over with you," he said, stepping into the hallway.

At the sight of him, she felt an unwanted nudge in the region of her heart. "If it's about the noises, we can talk freely. Alex is at Rosalie's."

Without taking his eyes off her, he pushed the door

closed behind him. "There is something I would like to do first."

Before she realized what was happening, she was in his arms and his mouth was firmly set on hers. The kiss softened into teasing nibbles that left her aching and breathless. Then, just as suddenly as he had taken her into his arms, he released her.

"That's your belated good-night kiss," he said huskily.

She stared at him numbly, her heart beating in her throat.

"I hope you slept better last night than I did," he said.

"I slept," she said simply.

"You talked too."

Her stomach kicked. "What did I say?"

"You said my name."

Her cheeks heated. "You're imagining things."

He shook his head slowly.

"What else did I say?"

"Isn't that enough?"

"If I did, you're reading something into it that wasn't there."

"I would hate to think that," he said playfully.

She took a deep breath to compose herself. "Stefan, you know that whatever there is between us is destined to go nowhere. I play for keeps and you don't. Home, hearth, and security are what I seek. They're what you avoid."

His mouth firmed into a straight line. "Let's not complicate things. Let's just make the best of now."

"When you have a child, you have to look beyond now," she countered.

He paced restlessly into the parlor. "Now is all that I can promise myself, let alone anyone else. I can only live for the moment, and I want those moments to count."

She'd always known that, but hearing him say it with such conviction filled her with a raw ache. It left a void more vast than she could have ever imagined.

"That idea that I wanted to discuss with you . . ." He changed the subject as easily as if his heart had an on-and-off switch. "I'd like to set up some monitoring devices in the upstairs bedrooms and in the attic so I can hear these noises for myself."

Alison blinked. "You're going to bug my house?"

"That's the idea."

After the initial surprise, she felt a twinge of relief. Better a monitor in her bedroom than Stephan. "I'll have to remember not to sing in the shower."

"Or talk in your sleep," he added.

She felt color crawl back up her cheeks.

"I'll get you set up over the weekend," he said with a businesslike tone. "Maybe we can get some answers and bring this story to an end."

What was between them would also end, she thought as she watched him leave. She knew it was for the best, but her heart seemed to have a mind of its own.

Chapter Nine

Alex followed Stefan from room to room like an adoring puppy as he put the monitoring devices into place. When Stefan finished, he carried Alex down the stairs on his shoulders. Alison noted that the boy's eyes were positively alight as he lifted him down. *You can toy with my heart*, she thought darkly, *but please don't hurt my son.*

"It's done," Stefan said. There were beads of perspiration at his temples. Dampened, his hair had fallen over his forehead. "If there's the slightest noise, that baby will pick it up."

"Thank you, Stefan," she said.

"Can we get a real baby?" Alex asked.

Alison's gaze snapped to her son. "Baby?"

He nodded.

Stefan, with one eyebrow cocked slightly, seemed to be eager to hear her answer. She felt her color deepen. "Where did you get such an idea, Alex?"

"Maybe I can shed some light on this," Stefan said. "I told him the devices were going to help us listen for squirrels and mice in the attic, that they worked a little like a baby monitor."

"Well, can we get a baby sometime?" Alex persisted. "Mikey's mother is getting one."

Stefan watched her, his eyes bright with playful anticipation. She shot him a look of caution before turning to Alex. "We can't have one without a daddy."

"What about Stefan?" he asked baldly.

An invisible hand seemed to grip her throat. She could feel Stefan's gaze burning into her. "Alex, don't forget your cartoon show," she said with stiff control. "Go on. It starts in a few minutes."

To her relief, the boy obediently scampered off into the parlor.

She turned awkwardly to Stefan, her cheeks tingling.

"I was wondering how we were going to get out of that one," he said.

"I'll talk to him later."

The smile in his eyes faded. An awkward pause followed.

"Alison, I'm going away for a while."

Her stomach tightened. "Where?"

"I volunteered for a special assignment."

"What kind of assignment?"

"I can't really tell you anything about it. The agency has a policy against discussing ongoing investigations."

Bewildered, all she could do for a moment was to

stare at him. His eyes were unreadable. "Is it danger-ous?"

His chin crinkled. "Life in general is dangerous."

She took in a sharp breath. "When are you leaving?"

"Tomorrow. I'm not sure when I'll be back—a few days, a few weeks—however long it takes."

Already she felt the ache of separation. "Please be careful."

"You watch out for ghosts," he said with a half smile. He reached out and brushed a strand of hair from her face. For a moment, his thumb lingered on her cheek, sending her heart leaping.

He stepped into the parlor to bid Alex a quick good-bye and then strode out without looking back.

The two guests came and went without incident, although the old professor said a waitress had told him about Lura Bea's ghost. "Amusing little story," he said with a laugh one afternoon while sipping tea. "But of course, who could believe in such nonsense?"

Half the town and a few visitors besides, Alison thought ruefully. It seemed that all anyone had to do was to mention that they were staying at the Prairie Flower and the story spilled out. At the rate word was getting around, her guests were going to dwindle to a trickle. She was beginning to wonder if buying the old house had been a huge and expensive mistake. And what was she going to tell Alex? She knew that sooner rather than later, she'd be forced to discuss the ghost with him.

A week passed and Stefan had still not returned.

Alex asked about him repeatedly. She worried about him constantly. She knew that life with Stefan would be just like this—marked by lonely vigils and nights clouded with fear. She also realized, with some alarm, that no matter where fate took each of them, she would always worry about him.

At nights, she lay awake listening for Lura Bea's "ghost," but all she heard was the distant whistle of a train and the occasional swoosh of a passing car. Then one night, she dropped off to sleep only to be startled awake. It was as if someone were in the room with her, looking down at the bed. A chill shot down her spine as she lay rigid. Her eyes strained at the dark, but she saw nothing but the dusky outlines of the furniture.

Suddenly, there was a sound. At first, it was barely audible, a strumming sound much like a step—a heel, then the ball of the foot against the floor. Alison's breath stalled in her chest. The noise grew louder. Then came another set of steplike noises, drawing closer. She bolted upright, her heart beating wildly in her chest. A soft cry tore out of her throat. "Alex?"

There was no answer, only a creaking sound that seemed to come vaguely from the direction of the attic stairs.

She flung her arm toward the bedside lamp, almost knocking the lamp over as she groped for the switch. She jumped out of bed to steady it and with trembling fingers, switched it on.

Light flooded the room, exposing the menace for what it was—nothing. There was no one there; no evidence anyone had been there. The clock at her bedside table read five minutes past midnight. She sat down on the bed. Her breath came in hard waves, and she pressed her hands to her chest to slow it.

Once she'd steadied herself, she walked softly to Alex's room. She found him sleeping soundly on his side, one foot stuck out from under the quilt. She gently covered it, then taking in a deep breath, she slowly ascended the attic stairs. Her heart hammering, she pushed open the door and switched on the light. Except for Alex's toys, the room was empty and bare.

Her knees wobbling, she went back to bed, but sleep eluded her for the rest of the night.

"Mom," Alex asked the next morning while digging into his cereal, "did you move my toys?"

Her heart banged against her ribs. "No. Why do you ask?"

"My puzzle was all messed up. And you know my airplane?"

"Of course, honey." The little airplane with the spinning plastic propellers was his favorite toy. He kept it in a place of honor on the attic window seat.

"It was on the floor," he continued.

Alison laid down her spoon. "Are you sure you didn't forget to put them away?"

"I'm sure," he insisted.

"I don't know, honey," she said, trying to sound unconcerned. "I'm sure there's a logical explanation for this. Maybe we have more mice."

He looked at her from under his thick crop of blond bangs and shook his head. "No, I think it's her."

Alison blinked in surprise. "Who?"

"The ghost."

She brought her hand to her mouth so suddenly that she accidentally tipped her bowl, spilling milk on the kitchen table. She slapped down her napkin to blot it up. "Alex, has somebody been telling you ghost stories?"

"I heard someone talking to Rosalie."

Alison didn't know whether to be relieved or horrified.

"But I knew there was a ghost before then," he said.

Her gaze riveted to his face. "Alex, how could you know? No one has ever seen a ghost."

"I just know, Mom. She's like a ghost in a cartoon. She plays with my toys while I'm asleep."

"She?"

He nodded. "She wants me to play with her, but I can't because I'm s'posed to be in bed."

"You've seen her?" she asked, incredulous.

"Nope. I just know she's there. She's a friendly ghost."

Alison stared at him. Was this a child's overactive imagination? Or had he made some kind of "connection" with a presence?

"Alex, you never said anything before now."

He put down his spoon and looked thoughtfully at her. "Well, I kept it a secret because I didn't want to scare you."

"Oh, Alex," she said, taking his small, sticky hand in hers, "but why are you telling me now?"

"Because I was hoping you moved my toys and that there really wasn't a ghost."

She went to his side, pulled him into her arms, and held him tight. "Alex, there *is* no ghost, not that anyone can see. Mice could have scattered your toys just like they did the last time. Please don't be afraid. There's an explanation for this."

He pulled away and gave her a baffled look. "I'm not afraid. I just wish she'd leave my toys alone."

She looked at him with amazement and frustration, wanting to laugh and cry at the same time. She was relieved that he wasn't frightened, or at least he pretended not to be, and frustrated because he persisted in believing there was a ghost. The more she tried to apply logic to the happenings, the more it seemed to fail her.

She could only be sure of this: Without paying guests, she would have trouble keeping the house. Who would want to buy a house, no matter how lovingly restored, as long as people, her own child included, believed it had a resident ghost?

The next day, the sky turned leaden and a whipping wind flung raindrops hard against the windows. Alison stepped out on the front porch to find the Boston ferns tossing about in their hanging planters and the pots of begonias all but rattling in their saucers. The porch swing creaked loudly.

Having taken Alex to a day camp, she was alone.

She'd been attempting to coax a shine out of the old kitchen floor when she heard the wind roar up. This was no ordinary thunderstorm.

The sky was streaked with grays and purples and lightning stitched through the horizon like a metallic thread. A rumble of thunder sent the floorboards humming under her sneakers. The noise was followed by a sudden curtain of rain.

Alison dashed back into the house and turned on the radio. "Severe thunderstorms, with possibly damaging winds of up to sixty miles an hour," it said. As of that moment, the "ghost" no longer mattered.

She ran upstairs and down, closing windows against the blowing rain. As she blotted water from an upstairs windowsill, she could see the limbs of the old oak in the front yard twist wildly. Amid the roar of the wind and rain was the sound of the doorbell.

She ran down the stairs. Stefan was standing on the porch, soaked. His hair was plastered to his forehead and droplets of water ran down his cheeks and down his windbreaker. His wet jeans clung to his legs. He was a mess, but Alison had never seen a more wonderful mess. She opened the door to him, barely managing to suppress the cry of relief that welled in her throat.

"Well, aren't you going to invite me in to drip all over your carpets?" His voice wrapped around her like a warm breeze.

"Oh, Stefan," was all she could manage to say.

She ran to the laundry room and came back with a stack of freshly washed towels. By then, he'd taken off his lace-up, military-style boots and parked them neatly on the welcome mat. He stepped inside and quickly toweled himself off. "At least you remember my name," he said.

She was so far beyond forgetting it that she'd never be quite the same. Seeing him again after a ten-day absence rekindled in her the sparks that she'd struggled so hard to extinguish. They leaped wildly in her veins, igniting into hundreds of little fires. Struggling to hide her feelings, she spoke to him in a controlled tone: "Come into the kitchen. I'll get you something hot to drink."

She got out the coffee grinder as he sat at the kitchen table. "Where have you been? Is everything O.K.?"

Before he could answer, a gust of wind slammed against the window so hard that Alison gasped. She dropped the grinder on the counter.

"It's okay." He got up and touched her arm. "The old house has seen worse."

She took a deep breath. "I haven't."

His mouth tightened into a straight line. "I figured as much. I heard the weather forecast after I got off the plane. When the wind got up, I thought I'd better stop here instead of going home. Being a three-story house, the Prairie Flower has taken some good hits in the past."

Alison stared at him dismally. "That too?"

"The good news is that it has been fixable—roof damage for the most part."

She sighed and turned back toward the window. It

was only mid-morning, but outside it was almost as dark as night. She eyed the blowing rain and envisioned her roof, or the entire house, spinning off into Kansas.

On the radio, an alert was issued for hail.

Stefan sat down. She was struck by his relative calmness. "Now, to answer your questions: First, I've been involved in a white-collar crime investigation. Second, I'm fine and I have some interesting news for you. But first, I want to know how it's been with you and Alex."

Alison switched on the coffeemaker, then turned toward him. "Stefan, I heard the noises again."

His eyes narrowed. "The same as before?"

She nodded, describing them in detail.

"I'll listen to the tape."

"I hope you will be able to hear it," she said, setting two steaming cups of coffee on the table. She added a plate of homemade chocolate chip cookies and sat down.

"If there were actual noises, they should have been picked up," he said.

"And Alex knows about the ghost," she added. "It's the strangest thing. He said he overheard Rosalie talking about it, but he says he knew before then. And he even claims she's a girl."

Stefan, who had lifted his cup halfway to his lips, set it down without tasting his coffee. He looked at her with such directness that she was startled.

"Is there something wrong?"

He rubbed his jaw. "Why don't we go sit in the parlor?"

Alison nodded, sensing that something was wrong. She quickly transferred the cups and saucers and the plate of cookies onto a tray. Stefan took it from her and followed her through the swinging kitchen door. She pulled an old wicker rocker across from the sofa and they sat with the coffee table between them.

"Alison, I know how concerned you've been about these noises and their effect on some of your guests, so I've been doing a little investigating in my spare time. I wanted to find out if the previous occupants of the house—and there was only one family—had had similar experiences.

"When I finished my work for the FBI a few days ago, I went to Texas, where I found one of the children who used to live here. He's ninety, hardly a child anymore, but he told me a lot of things about the house. When I add the information that you and Lura Bea have given me, it makes for a strange story."

Alison leaned forward, having almost forgotten about the rain and wind pelting against the house. "What do you mean?"

"Norbert Hartzel is the man's name. His father, a prosperous businessman, built the house. That's where he raised Norbert and his two sisters, Mildred and Frederica. Eighty years ago, at the age of seven, Frederica died in the room where you now sleep. Norbert told me that she had contracted whooping cough and that during the night, a maid attending her gave her the wrong kind of medicine. Frederica became violently ill and soon died from poisoning."

"What a tragic story," Alison interjected.

"Tragic and also very strange. The strangest part is yet to be told. Norbert said the attic was a playroom for him and his sisters, just as it is for Alex. It was full of toys and games and they often played up there at night before they had to go to bed. After they were put to bed, however, they would sneak back upstairs and continue to play, from about ten o'clock to midnight."

Alison brought her fingers to her lips. "That's when I hear the noises, the footsteps around my bed, the footsteps on the stairs."

"Should you want to believe in such things, maybe you can say that Frederica Hartzel is your little ghost."

She felt a chill.

"Norbert said the window seat where Alex likes to keep his toys was Frederica's favorite place."

"That's where his things were recently disturbed," she said in disbelief.

"What you mean?"

"He said his airplane had been moved from the window seat to the floor."

Contemplatively, Stefan scratched his stubbled jaw. "I think I might have the answer to that one. I may have moved it when I put up the monitoring devices."

Alison felt a wave of relief.

"But there's more," he continued. "He also told me that Frederica enjoyed books and music. Coincidence number two: Lura Bea complained about her books and music being out of order."

She stared numbly at him. "Stefan, please tell me you're making this up."

He shook his dark head slowly. She looked for the familiar dancing lights in his eyes. There were none. "I would consider Norbert Hartzel a credible witness. He may be old, but he's quite fit mentally. Physically too, I might add. He bowls three times a week with a senior citizen's league and zips around on a moped."

Alison blinked. "Stefan, what happened to your professional skepticism? Now, you're acting as if you believe this man. You didn't believe Lura Bea."

A grin teased his lips. "You were the one who thought there might be some credence to the ghost stories. Now, you're the skeptic."

She threw up her hands in frustration. "Stefan, I don't want to have a ghost. I want a nice, normal bed and breakfast where guests don't hear noises or cancel reservations because they're afraid they might."

"Don't think of her as a ghost. Think of her as a seven-year-old girl who visits occasionally. Just how scary can that be?"

Alison left her coffee unfinished and stood up on the worn Turkish carpet, rubbing her forehead. A cold, prickling sensation lingered along her spine. The spirit, if she could be called that, was a girl, just as Alex had said, one who loved to play with puzzles and toys. Using all the reason she could summon, Alison vigorously fought the notion of a ghost. But she couldn't categorically dismiss so many coincidences.

"Come here," Stefan said, patting a spot on the sofa. Hesitantly, she sat beside him.

"This house holds good memories for me, and it will for Alex too. One year, this house was on a special Christmas tour and Lura Bea had it so loaded down with garlands that I think about it every time I see a cedar tree. Every time I came, she always had something new and amusing for me—a game, a book, or a toy.

"To a small boy, the house was sort of a wonderland with all its nooks, crannies and vistas. I would go up into the attic, look out the window at all the trees and houses below and pretend I was the king of Cimarron. I imagined breaking the sound barrier as I slid down the banister."

Alison momentarily forgot about the little ghost and smiled. She imagined what a handsome boy Stefan must have been—sturdy and adventuresome.

He placed his arm on the back of the sofa and her blood stirred. His fingers were so near the nape of her neck that she could almost feel their heat.

"It was after my parents died that my attitude toward the house changed," he continued. "There I was, sixteen years old, sent to live with an eccentric old lady—not an adolescent boy's first choice as a housemate. It was quite an adjustment for me and for Lura Bea as well. My life had been shattered and hers disrupted. The house I'd associated with fun I began to associate with loss. But it's different with you and Alex here. You've made it bright, shiny, and full of life. Don't let a story—and just a story it may be—diminish that."

Alison glanced at the mantel with its framed *Home Sweet Home* cross-stitch, brass candlestick collection, and folk-painted fireplace screen. She'd created a cozy place for herself and her son. Signs of her love and labor were everywhere. Yet, ghost stories aside, it felt oddly lacking. She didn't have to look at the man beside her to know why.

Suddenly, she became aware that the rain had stopped and that the sky had brightened to a blue-gray. "The storm is over," she said, amazed at the relative calm.

"Let's go hear what your ghost sounds like," Stefan said. "Then we need to give the roof a quick check."

From her bedroom closet, he took a small apparatus electronically tied to the microphones that he had placed in the attic, in her room and in Alex's. Punching several switches, he located the sound on a micro-cassette. He listened closely, his lips pressed together in concentration. He rewound it and listened again. The strumming sounds of repeated footsteps were clearly audible.

Alison's mind clicked in recognition. "That's it."

"Interesting," he said.

"Do you believe me now?"

"Yes. There were obviously sounds. And they were very much like footsteps."

Alison placed her hands on her hips. "But you're not sure."

He shrugged. "We can never be sure unless we see someone or see footprints."

"And there we are back to the beginning of our vicious circle," she said. "No one has ever seen a ghost."

"Sorry to be so frustrating," he said, stuffing the small device into his pocket. "Let's go take a look at the shingles."

They went to the attic to a small window that opened out on a portion of the roof. Stefan took a long look, then moved aside so Alison could see. At first glance, all the shingles seemed to be intact. Emitting a brief sigh of relief, she stepped back and was closing the window when she heard the sound. Her nerves jumped. She reached back and grasped Stefan's arm. "I heard it again," she whispered loudly.

His gaze snapped to hers.

"Listen," she said.

For a few moments, she couldn't hear anything but the sound of her own breathing. Then it happened again.

Stefan gently nudged her aside and leaned out the window. The noise repeated itself.

Her heartbeat quickened. She scanned the attic, but saw nothing.

Suddenly, Stefan pulled back from the window. His mouth was slanted in a wry grin. "I think I've discovered the source of the noise."

Baffled, she looked at him. He hooked a hand around her waist and led her to the window. Holding her so close that she could feel him breathe, he pointed downward. "See that power line? Watch what happens when the wind blows."

The line, which entered the house just over Alison's bedroom window, strummed with the next gust of wind. "That's it!" she gasped. "That's the noise."

"That should account for some of your bumps in the night."

Alison's relief found escape in a giggle that wouldn't stop. Grinning, Stefan pulled her into his arms for a brief, celebratory hug. He released her, and then, as if he had second thoughts, he pulled her back against the lean length of him. She lifted her face and his mouth came down on hers with a fervor that made her dizzy. He paused to kiss the tip of her nose, to nuzzle her cheekbone, and then her temple. He came back to her lips once more for a final kiss, then released her.

She gazed into the murky gray depths of his eyes, too dazed to move. He dropped his hands from her sides and turned away from her. Her heart thundered in her chest.

Stefan took a few steps across the planks of the attic floor, then turned back toward her. "It seems that this case is closed." His tone was suddenly businesslike. "We can attribute some of the occurrences to the power line and to mice. The rest we can consign to your little ghost."

She stared at him uncomprehendingly. She'd barely absorbed what he'd said. "Stefan, you just kissed me."

He took a deep breath and let it out slowly. "You and I both know it would be best if we forgot that."

She felt a wrenching twist her gut. "No problem," she said, her voice tinged with irony.

He bit the inside of his cheek. "You and Alex deserve more than I can give."

A lump formed in her throat. She couldn't say he hadn't warned her.

"Now that the mystery is solved, I should go on to other things," he said with a weak smile.

"I understand," she said, struggling to keep her voice even. "Thank you for everything . . ." An awkward silence was broken by the sound of the doorbell. "It must be Rosalie with Alex," she said quickly.

Stefan followed her down the stairs. She opened the door to find Alex holding a rumpled finger painting of uncertain content. "He's all yours," Rosalie said with a dimpled smile, "and he's got a present for you."

While Alison thanked her, Alex ran excitedly past. "Oh, boy! Stefan's here!"

Stefan rumpled the boy's hair. "How's it going, pal?"

"We've got a ghost," he announced. "Here's a picture of her." He held up multicolored scribbles with a set of eyes.

Stefan raised an eyebrow. "She's quite a girl, all right. She doesn't scare you, does she?"

He shook his head adamantly. "Nope. She's nice."

Stefan glanced at Alison, his gaze containing a hint of amusement. "Sometime, when I come back, maybe you can introduce me."

"When are you coming back?" he asked.

"I don't know, Mr. Secret Agent. It may be awhile.

I've got some crooks to catch. Your mother has an inn to run. I won't be coming around as much. But when I'm in town, I'll stop by occasionally and check up on the spy business."

Alex produced a tight-lipped grin, the kind he wore he was trying to be brave.

"I'm going to ask you to take good care of your mother. Will you promise me you'll do that?"

The boy nodded earnestly.

"Good." Stefan gave his shoulder a squeeze, then rose to his full height. "I feel better already, knowing I'm leaving her in good hands."

He turned toward Alison, his expression unreadable. "I'd like to talk to you a few minutes if I can," he said softly.

A feeling of uneasiness stirred within her. She touched her son's head. "Alex, would you mind waiting for us on the porch swing?"

He hesitated for a moment, then trudged outside, his sneakers squeaking on the polished oak floor. Alison closed the front door and leaned against it. "What is it?"

Stefan put his hands in his pockets and squared his shoulders. The color in his eyes deepened to a somber gray. "Alison, I've put it for a transfer."

The room turned suddenly frigid. She stared at him, hoping she'd misunderstood. "You're leaving?"

He looked at her for a moment, then nodded. "There's a lot going on in the northern region right now. That's my first choice."

"But this is your home," she countered.

"This is the place where I lived. That's all. 'Home' is within me," he said stiffly.

An ache reached deeply inside her. "When are you going?" Her voice was weak.

"As soon as I'm approved. It could take a couple of weeks. It could take a couple of months."

She was so numb that she was barely breathing. "Alex will miss you," she said, fighting to maintain a composed facade. "And so will I."

His mouth tipped in a half smile. "I'll miss you too." He bent down and kissed her lightly on the cheekbone. Then, he was gone without another word.

Chapter Ten

She stood in the doorway and watched him leave. He paused on the front porch to ruffle Alex's hair.

"See you later, buddy." The afternoon sun rimmed his profile in gold.

Alex's face brightened. "Bye, Stefan." He bailed out of the porch swing, landing smoothly on both feet. "When are you coming back?"

There was a beat of silence. "Whenever I can," he said obliquely. Then he strode down the brick hedge-lined walk without looking back.

Alison's insides crumpled as she watched his long, fluid strides. His steps were brisk, like those of a man who had important things to do, important places to go, a man with a clear destination.

In leaving, he'd left a ringing emptiness. The sun seemed dimmer, the sky not quite so blue. The birds seemed to have fallen silent. The only sound was the porch swing creaking in the breeze.

"Alex, supper will be ready in about an hour," Alison said. She felt a need to reestablish a routine, to affect whatever normalcy she could.

He followed her into the parlor. "Mom, where's Stefan going?"

"Somewhere up north, maybe. He doesn't know for sure." She quickly changed the subject to his favorite meal. "How about some macaroni and cheese?"

"Okay," he said. His tone was flat.

"Run and play. I'll call you when it's done."

In the kitchen, Alison took a chunk of cheddar out of the refrigerator, but it might as well have been a moon rock. Instead of grating it, she sat down at the table and just stared at it. She remembered once wishing that Stefan would be assigned to the outer regions of Alaska. Now, her wish was being granted, more or less, save for a few degrees of latitude, and it didn't feel as good as she thought it would. In fact, it felt awful.

He wouldn't be here when she banged her thumb or when the ladder wasn't high enough to reach. He wouldn't be here to make Alex laugh or to give him a man's perspective on the world.

She picked up the cheese and set it back down with a thump. She didn't need him. She didn't need his smoky gaze or slanted smile, his perfect mouth or his imperfect nose. She didn't need his rich laughter or kisses filled with fire but devoid of lasting emotion. The two of them were wrong for each other; she was the homemaker, he was the happily homeless. They both knew it. They were going to settle for being buddies and now it seemed that even that turned out to be more than he wanted. With no warning, he was up and all but gone. So, who cared? The answer came in the form of a raw cry clawing at her throat.

She got up and attacked the cheese with a grater. Then she heard the piano. With uneven rhythm, Alex played the simple song that Stefan had taught him, each note reverberating through the house. Alison nicked a knuckle and winced. Alex began to sing the words to the song: "This is up. This is down. This is up and down."

Her mind turned back to Stefan at the piano those months ago as he played Chopin to lull Alex to sleep. At his fingers the notes rang sweet and pure, while at his side, there was his wagon—a forbidding flash of steel.

Alex played the song again, adding a riff of his own. The notes from the old baby grand floated through the kitchen door right into her heart. With a twisting little pain, the realization came: She was in love with Stefan. She was in love with a man who didn't love her and never would.

She looked around at the shabby kitchen and sighed so deeply that there seemed to be nothing left of her inside but a vacuum. She'd known better, so how could this have happened? Well, it had despite everything and she was going to have to live on—without Stefan.

The little song took on a mocking tone. Not wanting to hear it anymore, she pushed open the swinging kitchen door. "Alex, would you mind watering the plants on the front porch?"

His small hand dropped from the yellowed ivory keyboard. "Can I do it later? I'm playing a song."

"I'd appreciate it if you could do it now before we forget."

He swung his legs around and slid off the piano bench. "I can't reach the high ones," he said, referring to the hanging baskets, "but Stefan could. He can stand on his tip toes and almost touch the ceiling."

"Just water the ones in the pots," she said, ignoring the reference to Stefan. "I'll water the others."

She went back into the kitchen, but she found little relief from the piano's silence. A wildly dissonant tune continued inside her. It was a song of woe, of a little ghost who frightened guests and of a love that was all wrong.

Alison threw herself into the rest of the house with a fervor that almost left the walls vibrating. She tackled the upstairs hallway and her bedroom. She worked so hard that sleep—an escape from thoughts of Stefan—came easily.

Alex now knew about Frederica. He took the story with a quiet nonchalance. Alison tempered it with the more logical possibilities such as the humming power line, but Alex liked the idea of a secret ghost better.

Alison wished she could accept the story as happily. It gave Lura Bea's claims the credibility that had been lacking before. If the rumors had been bad for business, this new tale had the potential of being worse.

She spent hours worrying about it until one morning when the phone rang.

"Is it true that the Prairie Flower has a ghost?" a female caller asked.

Alison felt a twist of dismay. "That's the story," she said, sensing where her candor was going to lead.

"Wonderful!" the caller exclaimed. "I'd like to make a reservation for two."

Alison blinked. "You—you don't mind?"

"Not at all. In fact, my husband and I make a hobby of visiting places that are supposed to be haunted. We have great fun."

"Have you actually seen a ghost?" Alison asked.

"Well, no, but some people claim they have. Oh, it's so exciting. We just go and make a party of it."

At that moment, something inside Alison's mind took a leap, like an ember from a fire. It never occurred to her to have fun with the notion of a ghost, to allow people, including herself, to laugh at their fears.

An hour later, she was in a froth of excitement over the possibilities. She could plan special weekend events. There could be a formal dinner, followed by a night of acting out a script—a murder mystery. Guests could wear costumes from the Victorian era. The plot could contain a ghost.

She went to the computer, spending hours writing and deleting, then starting all over again. A story started to take shape, one with a maid who knew too much and a man who wanted to protect his secrets at any cost.

Also in her mind was another story, one of a man, a woman, and a little boy who wanted very much for the man to come back. The woman knew not to want what she couldn't have, but that didn't stop her from wanting it. She ached at the thought of him, the exquisitely delicate way his strong fingertips grazed her skin, the way his lips took possession of hers, the way he made her son's eyes light up and the world seem like magic.

Alison didn't need to contemplate the ending of that tale. She was living it one day at a time. For Alex's sake, she tried to do it with efficiency and cheer. But at night, she fell into bed exhausted from the strain of putting on a facade for her son and for the two guests who came that week.

After their first night, she told her visitors—one a young female stockbroker and the other, a pharmaceutical saleswoman—about the inn's legendary ghosts. They were more intrigued and amused than frightened. Of course, it helped considerably that no one had actually seen Frederica.

On Saturday, Alison went downtown to place an advertisement in the newspaper for the Prairie Flower's first "mystery" weekend. Once that was done, she took Alex for an ice cream cone at an old-fashioned parlor on Cimarron's Victorian Main Street. They sat down in vintage chairs of twisted wire. Alex happily plied into vanilla with multicolored sprinkles and Alison sampled cinnamon chocolate. They sat in front of the plate-glass window as ceiling fans whirled lazily overhead.

It was a nice spot for viewing the lovely old buildings across the street, except for one thing: One of the buildings was the Yale Hotel. On the fourth floor was Stefan's apartment.

"Look, there's Stefan!" Alex leaped from his seat and pressed his face into the window. A rivulet of ice cream formed where his cone touched the glass.

As she pulled him back, she saw Stefan and her heart stumbled. He stood in front of the hotel entrance for a moment, stopping briefly to buy a newspaper from a rack.

She was wiping up the sticky smudge that Alex had left on the window when a tall blond appeared in her range of vision. Her sleek hair grazed her shoulders and her shapely legs were sheathed in black Spandex shorts. She wore a matching black jogging halter, which, fell far short of covering her midsection, and she was bouncing right toward Stefan. Just as he turned from the news rack, she bounced up to him in her jogging shoes and kissed him briefly on the mouth. Alison experienced such a heavy sensation in her chest that she felt as if she'd swallowed a cannon ball.

"Who's that, Mom?" Alex asked.

"I don't know." Her voice was tight. "Sit down and eat your ice cream before it melts."

She sat across from him, deliberately placing her back to the window. She couldn't bear the pain of watching any longer. How much clearer could it be that she'd meant no more to him that a dozen other women, that he was a hopeless ladies' man?

"Mommy, you've got ice cream all over your hand."

Alison glanced down to see chocolate dripping from her cone and running down her fingers onto the table-top. Quickly, she blotted it up and finished the treat without tasting it.

"He's coming this way!" Alex jumped up out of his chair and ran toward the door.

Alison whirled to get a glimpse of Stefan, who was still on the opposite side of the street, but waiting at a nearby crosswalk. Suddenly, in her peripheral vision, she saw Alex darting out the door and onto the busy street.

"Alex, stop!" she screamed, making a grab for him, but it was too late. He had sprinted off the curb. He was running toward Stefan when an old Jeep suddenly careened around the corner at a high rate of speed.

At that instant, everything turned to slow motion. Alison watched in horror as Alex froze in the path of the oncoming vehicle. The driver hit his brakes, sending the Jeep weaving wildly. For what seemed to be an eternity, tires squealed and brakes squalled. Then came silence. The Jeep's front bumper came to a stop just inches away from Alex's chest.

Alison ran toward him, nearly faint with relief, and gathered him into her arms. Her heart thundered in her ears as she pulled him back to the sidewalk.

The Jeep's driver, a teenager with his baseball cap on backward and an earring in one ear, leaned out the open side of the vehicle. "Hey, kid, stay out of the road, would you? You could have caused me to mess up my Jeep."

Suddenly, a hand clamped down hard on the boy's

shoulder. Alison looked up to find Stefan, his eyes flashing with anger. "He's just a child," he said. "You failed to come to a complete stop and you were speeding. What's your excuse?"

"Hey, what are you, a cop or something?" the boy asked, sneering through a scraggly goatee.

Stefan reached into his back pocket, flipped his credentials open, and held them in front of the boy's face.

The youth shot him a look of resentment.

"Nothing is more valuable than a human life, yours included," Stefan said. "So, I advise you to get your priorities straight. And in thanksgiving that no one was hurt, vow to start driving more responsibly."

Meekly, the youth inched away but without an apology. Stefan took Alex from Alison's arms and held him tightly. "Are you all right, partner?" he asked softly.

The boy pulled back slightly, looked himself over and nodded. "No boo-boos."

"Good," Stefan said. The worry lines between his eyebrows softened. "You gave me quite a scare. What was your hurry?"

"I wanted to see you. You haven't come over for a big, long time."

Stefan's eyes met Alison's in a charged moment. Until then, she had been so focused on Alex that she'd all but forgotten the blond jogger. Suddenly, the scene replayed in her mind, sending a slicing pain through her heart.

"Well, Alex," Stefan said, tapping the boy's toy badge with his index finger, "I've been very busy. You know how it is with the spy business. But I haven't forgotten you or your mother and you have my promise that I won't."

Alison gave him a look of warning. *Please don't make promises you can't keep.*

Stefan set the boy down. "Are you all right, Alison?"

Her knees were still wobbling. "I will be."

"I'm sorry this happened," he said.

"It wasn't your fault." An awkward pause followed. She groped for Alex's hand. "We'd better go. Thank you for your concern."

"Alison . . ." he called as she started to turn. "I'd like to talk to you for a few minutes if I could."

She studied his face for a moment. His skin had taken on a golden hue from being outdoors. His hair was ruffled from the breeze.

"Let's stroll over to the park," he said. "Alex can play."

He took Alex's other hand and they walked in near silence the two blocks to a park with century-old trees, winding path, and a children's playground. "How's your little ghost friend?" Stefan asked finally.

"She's hiding," Alex said. "She hasn't been wanting to play."

"I see," he said, casting Alison a knowing look.

Alison was grateful that Stefan's attention was focused on Alex. It gave her a chance to wrestle with the turmoil inside her.

They turned Alex loose with some other children on one of several plastic zoo animals mounted on giant springs, and sat on a nearby park bench. To an old couple strolling by, she and Stefan must surely look like proud parents, Alison thought. How looks could deceive. How futile it was to even hope.

For a moment, they sat in silence watching the children. Alison gave her son an enthusiastic wave as he called to her from the top of a twisting slide, but inside, she was miserable. Stefan's handling of Alex's near-accident displayed some of the qualities that had led her to fall in love with him. Heaven knows, she hadn't wanted to.

They made small talk for a little while. Alison told him of the mystery weekend she'd planned and of the script she'd written. She wasn't sure what possessed her, but she invited him to the event and said he could bring a guest. She bantered on, even though her heart was cracking right in two, trying to pretend that they were nothing more than friends. It wasn't until he'd accepted without hesitation that she'd realized what she'd done. How could she get through the evening with Miss Spandex there?

"Look at me!" Alex yelled, breaking the silence that had fallen between them. He was hanging upside down from a row of bars.

She responded with two thumbs up.

"Alison . . ." There was something dark in Stefan's tone.

She turned toward him. The weekend stubble along his jaw made him achingly sexy.

"My transfer was approved."

The words slammed into her like a bus. For a moment, her tongue seemed locked into place. "Where will you be going?" she finally managed to ask.

"It looks like Montana." He told her without looking at her. A muscle worked in his jaw.

"That's what you wanted, wasn't it?" She spoke around a lump in her throat.

He glanced at her for a moment, nodding.

"I'm happy for you, then." A voice inside her told her she should consider his leaving a blessing. Out of sight, out of mind. She stared at the playground, refusing to look at his handsome face.

He sighed audibly. They were sitting close enough that she could almost feel his chest rise and fall. "I meant what I said about never forgetting you and Alex." He turned to her with a dark gaze that almost reached into her soul. "I want to keep in touch. I even expect to come back from time to time. There are people here who are important to me."

Alison's heart gave a hard twist. Surely, one was the woman in Spandex who had looked at him so adoringly.

"When are you leaving?

"In four weeks."

That seemed to Alison to be both an eternity and a split second. "It will be hard to break the news to Alex," she said with a strained voice. "He will be disappointed."

"I'll tell him if you like."

Alison shook her head. "It's all right. I will."

But it wasn't all right and it seemed like it would never be again.

*   *   *

Alex took the news with a predictable wash of tears. Afterward, Alison went into the kitchen where her own composure crumbled.

"But why does he have to go?" Alex had asked.

The answer had eluded her. Cimarron was Stefan's home and his past and he seemed compelled to separate himself from both. "Because he has some important work there." Not that his work here wasn't important too, but that was the best she could do.

The mystery-weekend project kept her properly focused. Shortly after she placed the ad in the newspaper, a reporter came and wrote a feature story on the Prairie Flower and Alison's plans. To her amazement, the weekend quickly sold out. A number of interested persons had to be turned down with a promise that another weekend would be scheduled as soon as possible.

Two special invitations had been issued, one to Rosalie, the other to Stefan. Rosalie had accepted immediately. There was no word from Stefan. Spending the evening in his presence, especially if he brought a guest, would rip her heart to pieces. But she couldn't not invite him. It was a matter of manners and pride.

A few nights later, after she'd put Alex to bed, she sat on the porch swing watching fireflies cavort in the darkness. Leaves of the old oak that framed the house rocked gently in the breeze. A glass of lemonade, rested on her knee, the ice long melted.

She'd spent the day carrying out a long list of things to do, from ordering the centerpiece, to mending some of the costumes that she'd bought at a used clothing store. She'd worn herself down to a numb exhaustion. It wasn't such a bad state to be in because it made it hard to think and hard to feel.

"Is there room on that swing for me too?"

The familiar baritone sent her blood leaping. She turned to find Stefan strolling up the brick walkway toward her.

She got up from the swing. "You surprised me."

He flashed one of those slanted smiles that always managed to turn her on her head. He held up a white card. She recognized it as the invitation she'd sent him. "I thought I'd respond in person. Thank you for inviting me. Yes, I'd very much like to come. Mysteries are sort of my specialty, you know."

"You're coming?" She was so tired that she was dizzy. Was the man standing before her real or was he a dream?

"Of course."

"Are you bringing someone?"

"Alison, I want to stop this nonsense. I've come for much more than just to accept an invitation." He encircled her elbow with his fingers.

Her skin tingled where he'd touched her. "What are you talking about?"

"Pretending we don't care for each other. I care for you; you care for me. Admit it."

She avoided his eyes. She knew she'd lose herself in them and she didn't want him to know how much she really cared. "No, Stefan, I won't admit it."

He took her chin in his hand and forced her to look

at him. His lips were inches from hers, causing her heart to strum wildly. "Look in my eyes and tell me you don't care," he demanded.

Stubbornly, she clamped her eyes shut so he couldn't see the tears forming in them. "Stop this, Stefan. I saw that woman kiss you in front of the hotel."

His hand dropped so suddenly that her eyes snapped open. He appeared stunned. "Alison," he said, his expression softening, "that was Collette, the kindergarten teacher and part-time model. She's getting married. She's so happy that she even kissed the desk clerk."

Alison blinked.

With his thumb, he wiped away a tear that had sneaked out of the corner of her eye. "I'd rather be kissed by you than anyone else."

She stared at him in disbelief. "Stefan, you're on your way to Montana. I don't understand."

He stepped back and ran a hand through his hair. "When I saw how close you and Alex came to being hit by that Jeep, the wall I'd built around myself just crumbled."

He took her by the shoulders again. His gaze was riveted to hers. "Do you know why I wanted to leave? Not for professional reasons, but because I wanted to distance myself from you. Now, I realize that I was running from my own heart and that no matter where I went, one fact would never change. I'm in love with you Alison."

Her heart went still. Even the cicadas seemed to stop buzzing.

"I've spent a good part of my life trying to guard

myself from any more losses. I've lost three people who meant everything to me—my parents and my partner. I figured after that that if I didn't love, I couldn't lose.

"I went from one woman to the next, not allowing myself the time to form a deep relationship. And it wasn't just because I didn't want to lose someone. I didn't want someone to lose me. So here I am, just the kind of man you don't need, and I'm telling you that I love you."

A lump formed in her throat. She reached out and touched his cheek. It was rough and heated. "I love you, Stefan."

He stared at her. "You really do?"

She nodded, unable to constrain the broad smile breaking out across her face.

He bent down and kissed it, then kissed her nose, her cheekbone and her temple. He kissed her mouth again with such exquisite lightness that her heart seemed to float out of her chest. "You know that loving me makes no sense at all. You've already lost one person you loved and here comes someone who could make you a widow all over again."

"I know, Stefan. But if I worry too much about the future, the present will be spoiled."

"I'll ask for less risky assignments. I'll do what I can to keep you from worrying too much about me."

"I don't want you to have to give up the job that you love."

"You know, there are lot of agents who retire without ever having to fire their weapons," he said. "Some have never even drawn them. We will work it out," he said. "I'll do anything I can to make you and Alex happy."

"Stefan, you mean so much to both of us."

He ran his fingers up and down her arm. "The funny thing is that we were two people trying to avoid more grief. Both of us were running and we ran right into each other. Now, what are we going to do about it?"

"I don't know," she whispered.

"I know," he said, tracing the outline of her lower lip with his thumb. "I want you to marry me."

Her lips parted. She was stunned wordless.

"I've already auditioned for the part," he said. "I'm very handy with a hammer and with little boys. I can fix a leaky faucet and I've been told I'm a good kisser."

A laugh bubbled from her throat.

"We'll stay here. You can keep the Prairie Flower and have all the eccentric guests you like."

"Stefan, yes. I'll marry you." She threw her arms around his neck.

He kissed her again. "Alison, I've been pursued and once, I was even fired at. None of that scared me as much as falling in love. Now I know that love has the power to conquer fear."

"Remember that I'm not the only one who loves you. Alex does too."

"Quite a threesome we'll be. Later, we might even become a foursome."

Her heart soared. "I'd like that."

He kissed her again. Her heart lifted like a balloon, toward a sky filled with endless possibilities.